Praise for

What You Have Left

by Will Allison

"One of Allison's greatest gifts is his ability to come at a story from an original, surprising angle. . . . Just as it seems clear where the story is going, Allison spins it in another direction, one that's somehow both surprising and inevitable. The moment is stunning. . . . he shows us a landscape that is rocky and difficult but that has its own sere beauty—the kind that, at the novel's best, can make us forget for a moment to inhale."

—*San Francisco Chronicle*

"[T]he novel's . . . characters slam through life embattled, weary, looking for missing pieces that most often remain missing."

—*The Los Angeles Times*

"Loss and redemption take center stage in storywriter Allison's beautifully written debut novel. Characters' tension-fraught relationships are well played, and Allison is adept at navigating a labyrinthine web of psychological underpinnings . . . the nonlinear narrative gives Allison a trove of angles, and he nails all of them.

—*Publishers Weekly,* starred review

"Soulful, salt-of-the-earth tales of hurt and hope in red-neck-proud South Carolina. . . . Raw-boned, heartfelt prose."

—*Kirkus,* starred review

"The novel takes its place on the shelf of American abandonment fiction. . . . In spare, transparent prose, Allison takes us through nearly four decades in the lives of a South Carolina family crippled by the past and unarmed for the future. . . . The strength of *What You Have Left* lies in the relationships among its characters. . . . Allison captures the truth and irony of being part of a family, no matter how broken it is."

—*The Washington Post*

"Allison knows Southern characters and paints them with a sympathetic brush, even when they're addicted to video poker, sneaking cigarettes, or defending their state's right to fly the Confederate flag. *What You Have Left* is a book readers will want to rush through and savor at the same time."

—*Bookpage*

"Allison's engaging debut dissects the guilt and betrayal embedded in the history of one South Carolina family. . . . Allison clearly empathizes with his characters' foibles and manages always to find some measure of humor when they repeatedly let each other down."

—*Booklist*

"Allison has crafted the sort of novel that should find a home in book groups everywhere."

—*Edmonton Journal*

"[A]n enchanting, winsome look at Southern life . . . [the novel] concerns the sundry and tenuous bonds of family, with the specter of auto racing, NASCAR-style, buzzing in the background."

—*Pittsburgh Tribune-Review*

"Allison's writing exposes brutal honesty with grace. Holly, Wylie, and Lyle know we're hearing them out—sort of like poker players dealing the cards to their lives, daring us to show our hand to trump or fold."

—*NUVO*, Indianapolis

"The moving account tells of a South Carolina family struggling to survive despite a mother's death, a father's abandonment, and a grandfather's battle with Alzheimer's disease—and a host of risky behaviors by others left behind."
—*Columbus Dispatch*

"Allison does not tug at the heart with his narrative but rather takes up the threads of his characters' lives with patience and a keen eye for the telling of detail."
—*Charleston City Paper*

"Allison's writing is personal and direct, his characters are interesting but not quirky."
—*Library Journal*

"A remarkably cohesive novel in which the chapters also can stand alone as stories."
—*This Week,* Ohio

"Allison structures his book well, writes in significantly understated but poignant prose, and keeps the reader riveted."
—*Southern Seen*

"Propelled by Allison's spare, straightforward prose, *What You Have Left* looks at the often uncomfortable circumstances of facing one's past mistakes and the peculiar tapestry of American lives in the late-20th century with keen insight and genuine feeling."
—*City Beat*

"Allison capably explores the enduring bonds that link family together."
—*The Independent Weekly*
(Raleigh, Durham, Chapel Hill)

"*What You Have Left* is a remarkable first novel that glows with feeling and crackles with surprising insight into the ways that families shape one another. I love the elegance of Will Allison's prose—he knows how to write a beautiful sentence but hasn't forgotten how to tell a story too—and his book shows such wonderful control over complex moods: it's funny yet thoughtful, heartfelt yet unsentimental, and altogether a rich and rewarding reading experience."

—Dan Chaon, author of
Await Your Reply

"Will Allison's *What You Have Left* is written with such vitality, such delicate intensity and clarity of feeling that I wanted it never to end. A story of fast cars and colliding emotions, it runs quicker than a dirt-track car on a Saturday night. The characters are heartbreaking, and absolutely real—good people spinning out of control."

—Mark Childress, author of
Georgia Bottoms

"The clarity of Will Allison's prose underscores the small, crucial moments when the fate of human beings is decided, on the subtle abacus of hope and accommodation, betrayal and love. He perfectly captures the texture of unstylized American lives."

—Janet Fitch, author of
White Oleander and *Paint It Black*

"The death of race car driver Maddy Greer reverberates through the interlocking chapters of *What You Have Left,* creating a sharp and haunting picture of an absence. The prose is precise, the observations acute, and the emotional range huge. This is beautiful work."

—Karen Joy Fowler, author of
The Jane Austen Book Club

"Though the beautifully drawn characters of Will Allison's *What You Have Left* do not understand how their lives draft, fender to bumper, upon each other, the reader can only sit back wondering whether clear driving's ahead, or a seemingly inevitable disaster. This is a masterpiece in writing, and in understanding Nature versus Nuture. We understand that Holly's her mother and father's child whether she wants to be or not, and know that, in time, the little firecracker Claire will be her own independent-thinking, stock car driving, wonderfully obsessed person in her own right. Brutally hilarious and mesmerically tragic, *What You Have Left* might be the perfect novel. These characters will be sticking to my ribs for years."

—George Singleton, author of *Work Shirts for Madmen*

"No matter where you're from, Will Allison's novel feels like home, with characters who challenge, defy, and love each other in the ways that every family must. All that plus stock car racing—what's not to love?"

—Erika Krouse, author of *Come Up and See Me Sometime*

WHAT
YOU HAVE
LEFT

A Novel

WILL ALLISON

FREE PRESS
New York London Toronto Sydney

FREE PRESS
A Division of Simon & Schuster, Inc.
1230 Avenue of the Americas
New York, NY 10020

This Free Press trade paperback edition February 2011

Portions of this novel have appeared or are forthcoming in the following
publications: *Glimmer Train* (Issue #61, Winter 2007), *Cincinnati Review* (Fall
2006), *One Story* (Issue #47, November 2004), *Zoetrope: All-Story* (Vol. 8, No. 2,
Summer 2004), *Atlanta Magazine* (Vol. 44, No. 1, May 2004), *Kenyon Review*
(Vol. XXVI, No. 2, 2003), *Shenandoah* (Vol. 52, No. 1, Spring 2002).

FREE PRESS and colophon are trademarks of Simon & Schuster, Inc.

For information about special discounts for bulk purchases,
please contact Simon & Schuster Special Sales at 1-866-506-1949
or business@simonandschuster.com

The Simon & Schuster Speakers Bureau can bring authors
to your live event. For more information or to book an event
contact the Simon & Schuster Speakers Bureau at 1-866-248-3049
or visit our website at www.simonspeakers.com

Manufactured in the United States of America

10 9 8 7 6 5 4 3 2 1

Library of Congress Cataloging-in-Publication
Data Control Number: 2006051876

ISBN 978-1-4516-4319-0
ISBN 978-1-4165-4319-0 (pbk)
ISBN 978-1-4165-4667-2 (ebook)

For Deborah, who made me start over

CONTENTS

CHAPTER ONE

1991

Holly

I was sentenced to life on my grandfather's dairy farm in the summer of 1976. The arrangement was supposed to be temporary, a month or so until my mother recovered from her water-skiing accident, but after one week, on the first day she was able to get out of her hospital bed and walk, a blood clot traveled up from her leg, blocked the vessels to her lungs, and killed her. My father had been the one driving the boat, the one who steered too close to the dock. Three days after the funeral, he walked out of the insurance agency where he worked and wasn't heard from again.

Though my grandfather, Cal, spent months trying to track him down, it was no use, and that's how, at the age of five, I came to be spending my nights in the bed my mother had slept in as a child. Cal made a gift to me of my mother's arrowhead collection, which he'd helped her assemble when she was little. He also decided to repaint her bedroom for me and said I could pick the color. He was trying to be nice, but I wasn't ready for nice. At Taylor Hardware, I chose Day-Glo orange, held the sample card up for my grandfather's approval, and then proceeded to pick out three more hideous shades of orange—one for each wall—daring him to say no. Instead of stopping me, instead of telling me one color would do, he'd simply nodded. "Anything you want, sugar plum," he said. Naturally, I threw a tantrum. What I wanted was my mom and dad, not stupid paint for a stupid room in a stupid old farmhouse. I'm sure everyone in the store thought I had it coming, but rather than drag me out to the parking lot for a spanking, as he'd surely have done with my mother, Cal just picked me up and held on as I kicked.

My grandfather's relationship with my mother, his only child, was a difficult one, and the subject of her death always left him at a loss. Whenever I asked about her, Cal would either fall silent or try to deflect my questions with anodyne bits of wisdom, mostly quotations from the tattered *Bartlett's* he kept by the toilet. His standby, the old chestnut that exasperated me most, was a line from Hubert Humphrey: "My friend, it's not what they take away from you that counts; it's what you do with what you have left."

At the time, of course, I was too young to appreciate what my grandfather was doing with what he had left— raising yours truly—and in all my worry over what had been taken from me, I failed to consider how much had been taken from him. My grandmother, Josie, had passed away before I was born, and shortly after my mother's death, my great-grandfather died as well. The Colonel had been living in the Alzheimer's ward of a nursing home in Blythewood, a low brick building that smelled of Pine-Sol and pea soup. I hated visiting him, but Cal always brought me along, telling me that one day I'd be glad I'd gotten to know my great-grandfather.

There wasn't much left to know. During our visits, the

attendant would park the Colonel's wheelchair by the window, where the sunlight lent his eyes a misleading sparkle. On the rare occasions he addressed me, he called me by my mother's name, Maddy, but usually he'd just grab my wrist and shake it, moaning, *oh oh oh*. Looking back on those visits, I now see that if they were unpleasant for me, they were torture for Cal, who wasn't just seeing his father; he was seeing his own future self. Over the years, he'd watched his grandfather, his uncle, and now the Colonel succumb to the same disease—smart, willful men reduced to drooling and diapers. He'd seen the ugliness of it, the anvil weight on his family, and he was determined not to go down the same road. Driving home from the Colonel's funeral, he took a long swallow from his silver flask and swore he'd take matters into his own hands before it came to that.

I never forgot that vow, though when I was old enough to understand what it meant, I told myself it was just talk, that my grandfather would never intentionally leave me. But in the end, Cal was true to his word. When his mind started to go, he fought back with a handful of sleeping pills, leaving me the farm where I now live with my husband, Lyle, who was hired to renovate the farmhouse in the months before Cal's death.

My grandfather first told me he was sick during the spring of my sophomore year at Carolina. He was starting to slip, was how he put it. "Maybe it's something and maybe it's not," he said. "The doctors don't know for sure yet." It was early April, and I was at the farm for our weekly cocktails, the two of us sitting out front beneath the mossy live oaks, a pitcher of Cal's peppery bloody marys on the wrought-iron table between us. I watched Lyle and his crew stacking steel beams alongside the house as Cal told me that over the past few months, he'd begun forgetting things—names, appointments, the day of the week. He figured it was probably old age, no reason to get all bent out of shape, but just to be safe, he'd gone to the VA for a checkup. They'd given him a physical and a mental-status evaluation. Now they wanted him back for more tests. I stared into my drink, thinking about how he'd forgotten my birthday that fall, how I'd been so busy with classes and pledge meetings that I blew it off, even though it was exactly the sort of lapse I'd always been on the lookout for. Cal patted my knee and told me to cheer up. "Like Yogi Berra said, it ain't over till it's over." Then he stared into his drink, too. "Course, he also said the future ain't what it used to be."

The pecky-cypress paneling in the master bedroom of our house is pitted and scarred, the handiwork of a thousand woodpeckers, or at least that's what I imagined as a five-year-old. When I'd asked Cal about his funny-looking walls, though, he told me the pockmarks weren't the result of woodpeckers or worms or beetles, as many people believed, but rather a rare and little-understood fungus. "What makes pecky hard to find," he said, "is that you can't tell if a cypress is infected until you chop down the tree and cut it open."

When he'd purchased the farm, in 1939, the house wasn't a house, it was a grain barn. He divided the building into rooms and framed doors and windows using wood from an old sharecropper's cabin. After that first drafty winter, Josie shivering next to him in bed, he decided to insulate and panel their bedroom walls. He originally thought he'd get the wood from the Colonel's sawmill, but this was the Depression: Cal couldn't afford to buy lumber, and the Colonel couldn't afford to give it away, not even to his own son. The best he could do was let Cal help himself to the scrap pile, which was where he found, underneath an old tarp, a load of pecky cypress, enough to panel the bedroom and his workshop. In later years, people would develop a taste for pecky and an appreciation for its scarcity, but in those days, it was considered junk wood. Josie didn't care; she said it had low-country charm. Mainly, though, she was pleased that Cal went to all that trouble for her even as he worked twelve-hour days trying to establish their dairy farm. Her gratitude was not lost on him, and for the rest of her life, whenever he wanted to please her, he embarked on some new project to make the house more comfortable. Just before my mother was born, he added on a whole second story, and in later years he expanded the dining room and added a built-in china cabinet, then converted the front porch into a sitting parlor with French doors. In 1969, he was halfway done painting the house a minty shade of green that Josie picked out when doctors discovered the tumor in her breast.

After Josie's death, my grandfather let the house fall into disrepair, but during the fall of my sophomore year, when he first began having trouble with his memory, he sold off several parcels of land and started using the money to fix the place up. Though I didn't know it at the time, he did this for me, for when I inherited the farm.

At seventy-two, he was no longer able to do the work himself, so he hired Lyle on the recommendation of an old army buddy. In those days, Lyle was more handyman than general contractor, but he worked cheap, and my grandfather liked his manners, the fact that his family was well off, the fact that he'd been smart enough for grad school but then turned his back on all that academic baloney. Inside a month, Cal was inviting him to join us for happy hour. By then I already had my eye on Lyle—a shirtless guy tuck-pointing a chimney apparently being one of my weaknesses—but he seemed more interested in Cal's company than mine, so I played it close to the chest.

That all changed on the afternoon my grandfather told me he was sick. He'd just finished filling me in on his visit to the VA when Lyle and the two guys who worked for him came crawling out from under the house, brushing soil from their jeans. That week they were trying to fix the sloping floor in the living room. The joists beneath the oak floorboards were supported by heavy girders cut from the heartwood of long-leaf pines, and their plan was to reinforce these girders with steel beams, jack them up, and then build concrete pillars to stabilize the floor. After his crew knocked off for the day, Lyle joined us and began to report on their progress, and soon talk turned to the next project, a new roof. My grandfather didn't mention his health again, but I could think of nothing else, and as he and Lyle droned on about shingles and soffits, I stared out at the fields that once fed Cal's registered Guernseys and quietly plowed my way through two more drinks.

When the sun started to dip behind the bluff, Cal left for his monthly poker game at the country club; as he drove down the lane, he flashed us the peace sign, something he'd picked up from Lyle. Once he was gone, I lit a smoke and emptied the last of the pitcher into my glass. "You ought to make sure he pays you before he blows his brains out," I said.

Lyle smiled, then quit smiling when he saw I was serious, then smiled again because he didn't know what else to do.

"Come again?"

I sent him inside to mix another pitcher, and when he returned, I continued to get embarrassingly drunk and told him everything, all the while vaguely aware that I was trying to seduce him, never mind that he was twenty-four and I was only nineteen. When I got around to the part about Cal planning to "take matters into his own hands," Lyle was doubtful. "Isn't that just something people say? To give themselves a sense of control?"

"You don't know my grandfather," I said. I hoped Lyle was right, though. It had always terrified me to think Cal would end up like the Colonel, but even that would have been better than no Cal at all. Still, the few times he'd alluded to killing himself—usually in the fading twilight of a vodka-soaked cocktail hour, and usually in the context of what his father ought to have done—I'd simply nodded along, trying to maintain the sort of grown-up composure he admired. I understood, even as a child, that I was always being compared to my mother, contrary, contentious, confounding Maddy. "You," he'd say, tousling my hair, "you I don't have to worry about."

But of course he worried anyway, and as I sat there with Lyle, listening to the crickets and watching the Spanish moss flutter in the breeze, I began to understand why Cal kept inviting him to join us: He was worried about what would happen to me after he was gone. He was worried about me being alone. By now I'd started to get weepy, and Lyle put an arm around me, telling me things would work out. The fireflies were just starting to appear as I took his hand and led him into the house, through the French doors of the parlor, past the pocked paneling of the workshop, and upstairs to the bedroom with faded Day-Glo walls and the curio cabinet lined with my mother's arrowheads.

A few days before semester's end, Cal was scheduled for a neurological exam at the VA, but he missed the appointment. Dr. Miller assumed he'd forgotten—a symptomatic memory lapse—but I chalked it up to my grandfather's dislike of hospitals, and who could blame him, given the way things had turned out with Josie and my mother? It was decided that I'd take him to his next appointment. On a Tuesday morning in early May, I hurried through a biology exam and then drove out to the farm. When I arrived, I found Cal in his workshop, a stifling, narrow room crowded with fishing poles, hand tools, gardening tools, faded seed packets, scraps of sandpaper, bits of wood, rusted Folgers cans filled with nails, screws, washers, nuts, and bolts. He invited me in. On his workbench was a brown prescription bottle; he'd been grinding up pills with the porcelain mortar and pestle he'd once used to mix medicine for livestock. As he poured the powder back into the bottle, he said that if it turned out he was sick—and nobody was saying for sure he was, don't go burying him yet—but *if* he was, this was how he'd do it. Sleeping pills. Twenty of them dissolved in a stiff drink were guaranteed to do the trick. I picked up one of the bottles and examined the label, feeling suddenly hot and dizzy, as if I'd just downed a handful of pills myself.

"Why not just use a shotgun?"

"And mess up this pretty face?" Cal tapped his watch and turned to go: We didn't want to miss another appointment.

• • •

In spite of the tough-girl act I put on for Cal, I never could stomach what passed for mercy on a farm. Over the years, I saw him put down more animals than I care to remember: sick cows, sick goats, and sick chickens; rabbits maimed by cats, cats mauled by dogs, dogs hit by cars. "You don't let a suffering thing suffer," he'd say. One hazy morning when I was ten, I went to the mailbox and found our coon dog, Leopold, lying in a ditch beside the highway, bleeding from the mouth. His ribs quivered as if he were torn between the need for air and the pain of breathing. My grandfather brought his shotgun, took one look at Leo, and did what needed to be done. When I heard the gunshot, what I felt was relief, but also a kind of hatred.

Lyle stood in the middle of my grandfather's workshop admiring the pecky cypress while I rifled the shelves above the workbench. "You know what this stuff is worth?" he said, tracing a finger along the pale wood.

"He got it for free," I said. "Ask him. He loves to tell the story." When I didn't find what I was looking for on the shelves, I checked the window to make sure Cal was still practicing his golf swing, then moved on to his tackle box. As I scanned the trays of iridescent flies, Lyle told me about a friend of his whose father once owned a lumber mill up in Spartanburg. He said that when they cut open a cypress and discovered it was pecky, they used to shut down the whole operation, drive that one tree to market, and split the profits. "Then they'd take the rest of the day off," he said. "All thanks to some worms."

The pill bottle was hidden among spools of fishing line in the bottom of the tackle box. I handed it to Lyle. He unscrewed the cap and looked inside, frowning. For a minute or two we just stood there, listening to the sounds of his crew tearing off the old roof, the hollow pop of Cal giving flight to another ball. Finally Lyle said, "So what are you going to do?" I'd been hoping he'd insist we talk to Cal, take away his pills, put him in a nursing home if that's what it took, but Lyle just stood there squinting in the hard light that slanted through the window, looking like he wished he were someplace else.

"You don't think I should do anything, do you?"

"I didn't say that," Lyle said. "But it is *his* life, right?"

I put the pill bottle back in the tackle box and pushed past him on my way out. He caught up with me in the kitchen pouring a shot of whiskey. When he started to apologize, I cut him off. "And the worms in pecky cypress?" I said. "Any idiot knows it's a fungus."

The neurological exam raised red flags, so the next week, I took Cal in for a dizzying alphabet of tests—EEG, CT, MRI, PET, SPECT. Then it was back to the psychiatrist, this time for neuropsychological screening, a series of interviews and written tests that left Cal exhausted and irritable. Dr. Miller kept telling us it was a process of elimination; they had to rule out a thyroid problem, stroke, depression.

By the time it came, the diagnosis was no surprise. "Dementia," Dr. Miller said, "of the Alzheimer type." We were sitting in his office at the VA. Cal didn't even blink. "Of the type, huh? You sure you got the right type?" Dr. Miller understood that he was being mocked, but he kept his cool, explaining yet again that an educated guess was the best he could do.

I'd learned all about Alzheimer's in middle school, when I studied up on it in the school library. I read about the change that occurs in the brain, the formation of a mysterious, gummy plaque whose presence can be verified only by autopsy. It had made me think of our pecky cypress walls, and sometimes I imagined my grandfather dead on a conveyor belt, a buzz saw slicing into his head as curious lumberjacks leaned in for a look. Of course, whereas a pecky cypress shows no external signs of its illness, an Alzheimer's patient shows plenty, so I'd compiled a list of warning signs in my notebook—memory loss, difficulty performing familiar tasks, problems with language, changes in mood or behavior, etc. For years I watched my grandfather and waited, ready for doom every time he so much as misplaced his keys or confused the names of my friends.

And now that the dark clouds on the horizon had finally rolled in, I found myself facing an even worse wait. The doctors told Cal he might last three years or he might last twenty, but Cal knew that in our family, the disease tended to hit hard and fast, and he seemed determined not to put things off. It made sense that he'd want to take care of business now, while he still had the presence of mind to do so. The day after he was diagnosed, he met with his lawyer about putting his affairs in order, and that weekend he made clear to me that he wanted to finish work on the house as soon as possible. "How soon?" I asked him. It was after the end of spring semester, a Saturday morning, and we were unloading boxes into the swaybacked barn that once sheltered his farming equipment—tractor, sickle mower, silage chopper, disc harrow, bottom plow. The cannibalized

13

remains of an old combine still filled one corner, but the other machines were gone, sold at auction in 1977, the year Cal buried the Colonel and herded his cows between the milking parlor's stanchions for the last time.

"End of summer," he said. "Labor Day at the latest."

"That's not much time."

"Lyle'll manage," Cal said, lifting another box from the pickup and piling it onto a wooden pallet alongside the combine. We'd been clearing out the attic so Lyle's crew could add new insulation, and we were down to the last load, mostly boxes containing my mother's belongings. After my father skipped town, Cal had gone to the little lake house where we lived, packed her stuff, and stowed everything in the attic. As a child, I wasn't supposed to go up there—Cal told me there were bats—but that never stopped me. I'd spent hours going through her clothes, poring over her photo albums and scrapbooks. Now, rearranging the boxes on the pallet, my arms felt dead, like elastic bands that had lost their snap. Cal was tireless, though. His sun-leathered hands looked as if they could still wrestle a breech calf from a panicked heifer. While he went back to the truck, I took a breather, digging through a box until I found my mother's wedding dress in its plastic dry cleaner's bag. It was more sundress than wedding gown, a bit too Summer of Love for my taste, but as I held it against me and swished from side to side, I could see its appeal. When I glanced up, Cal was standing in the doorway of the barn, a wistful smile on his face. "You know, I never did think I'd see you in a wedding dress."

"And maybe you never will," I said. I was hoping to hurt him a little, to remind him what he had to live for, but Cal just seemed confused. He started to say something and then

14

stopped, staring at me as if I were a familiar face he couldn't quite place. It wasn't until he turned back to the truck, clearly shaken, that I understood it wasn't me he'd been talking to.

I moved back to the farm the following weekend. Cal tried to talk me out of it, suggesting I stay put in the sorority house, but I said I wanted to spend more time with him, and he couldn't argue with that. For the first few weeks, life wasn't so different than it had been the previous summer. The doctors had fine-tuned Cal's medication, and it was possible, watching him peruse the newspaper or tie a fishing lure, to imagine his diagnosis had simply been wrong. Then June melted away into July, and the blast-furnace heat of midsummer seemed to slow everything down, including Cal. Simple conversation began to confound him, his thoughts like knotted rope, and twice he got lost driving in town, unable to solve the once-familiar streets. Determined not to embarrass himself, he gave up his poker game, turned down fishing trips, stopped answering the phone.

We continued our Friday cocktails against doctor's orders, but even with Lyle there, those evenings were strained. I'd never realized how much you talk about the future until the topic was off limits. With nowhere to be, Cal invariably ended up drunk. Lyle encouraged me to water down his drinks, but instead I poured him doubles, so he'd sleep sooner. By then I was spending two or three nights a week at Lyle's apartment, hurrying home each morning so I could have grits and toast waiting on the table for Cal. After breakfast, he'd spend a few hours doing whatever he could to help Lyle, but the afternoons were ours. When we finished lunch, usually leftover fried chicken or barbecue sandwiches bought for the workers, we'd head out to his makeshift driving range, a onetime soybean field he'd seeded with Kentucky bluegrass after he gave up farming. For years he'd been wanting to teach me golf; now I took him up on his offer. We'd start by walking the range together, gathering balls in an old milk pail, and then he'd coach me until the afternoon sun drove us inside, all the while fielding questions about my mother and Josie as I worked to keep his memory sharp. I wasn't really expecting to hear anything new, but after fifteen years of mostly dodging the subject, Cal surprised me by talking more frankly about his problems with my mother. In between pointed critiques of my grip and stance, he confessed to having been overly protective and overly strict, not letting my mother live her own life, as she used to say to him.

The trouble between Cal and my mother started when she came down with rheumatic fever. She was seven years old, and the doctor said she'd be crippled for life if her heart wasn't given sufficient time to heal. He ordered six weeks bed rest. She was not to get up at all—Cal and Josie would feed her, bathe her, change her clothes, even take her to the bathroom.

That was 1954, the summer Cal tore down the old barn and built a new one. One of the farmhands, Willie Jones, used to ferry my mother around on his shoulders while she was sick. Sometimes he'd set her on a blanket under the chinaberry tree so she could watch the barn rising in the field. The chief carpenter, Old Man Carey, carried a bar of Octagon soap in his pocket, and with the help of Cal's binoculars, she'd study the way he soaped each nail before driving it into the boards of hard, green oak.

One afternoon, my mother got restless. She couldn't lie in bed examining her arrowheads one minute longer. Sneaking downstairs, she bumped into Josie coming inside with a basket of laundry. Normally, Josie was in charge of discipline, but this was such a serious offense that she summoned Cal from the fields. He carried my mother back upstairs, held her in the air by her wrists, and beat her with his belt, determined that his daughter would not end up a cripple. My mother was so upset she stopped speaking to him, even though that meant wetting the bed while she waited for Josie to return from market. At the time, Cal tried not to trouble himself much about the whole episode. He was sure she'd forgive him when she was older, when she could see he'd done it for her own good.

Labor Day came and went, and still Lyle worked on the house. His final project was to paint the exterior, a huge job that involved scraping off the old paint, repairing broken clapboards, sanding the wood, treating it with a mixture of linseed oil and turpentine, and then finally priming and painting. He hired a third man, but even with the extra help, the job took longer than expected. They worked every day, six days a week, starting at dawn. Sometimes they attached floodlights to the scaffolding and worked into the evening. I begged him to slow down, but Cal was pushing him to finish. "What am I supposed to do?" Lyle said. "He wants it done yesterday."

I'd taken the semester off to stay home full-time with Cal. His spells had worsened, and he was growing more anxious by the day. I reminded him that treatment had gotten a lot better since the Colonel's time, that some doctors even believed a cure was near, but it was clear he just wanted to get it over with. After my golf lesson, he often had me drive him to the cemetery, where he stood at the graves of my mother and Josie, telling them, I imagined, that he'd be with them soon.

It was late September when Lyle finally sealed the last bucket of paint and dismantled the scaffolding. That afternoon, my grandfather was to meet with his attorney to finalize his will. As the two of us stood in the yard admiring the house, I told him he should leave the farm to his sister, who lived out West. "The house, the land, whatever," I said. "I don't want it." He fixed me with a fierce look: There I was, the one person who mattered to him, making things even harder. But I didn't care. He was hurting me, and I wanted him to know it. He told me he and Josie had worked all their lives to make sure my mother would be taken care of once they were gone. "You're her daughter," he said, "so like it or not, it's all coming to you."

When the lawyer arrived, I slipped into Cal's workshop, pocketed the pill bottle from his tackle box, and told him I needed to run some errands. My plan was to see Dr. Miller and tell him what Cal intended to do, but after an hour in the parking lot at the VA, staring at the pill bottle on my dashboard, I lost my nerve imagining the look on Cal's face if he found out I betrayed him to a doctor. I spent the rest of the day driving around with a pint of vodka between my knees, eventually making my way out to Lexington, across the dam to Irmo, and then up Highway 5 toward White Rock. I wanted to see the little lake house where I'd lived with my parents before my mother's accident. I hadn't been there in years, and at first I thought I'd made a wrong turn in the shadowy dusk. But it turned out the house was gone, as were the other cottages that had once dotted the shore, and in their place stood a row of condominiums overlooking the lake. Also gone was our rickety dock. Now five new docks pointed like fingers into the cove, each one ringed by expensive-looking sailboats.

By then, of course, it had begun to rain. For weeks I'd been praying for a storm, rain being the only thing that would have slowed Lyle's crew, but the late summer sky had stayed clear and blue. Lights shone in a couple of the condos; figuring the weather would keep people inside, I took a seat at the end of a dock, letting my feet dangle in the water. Across the lake, lightning speared the sky.

My mother's accident happened on the day after the Fourth of July. The night before, she and my father had hosted their annual cookout, a big bash that involved a bonfire, several coolers of Schlitz, roman candles, and loud music from the eight-track player in my father's Firebird, which he parked near the lake's edge. While the grown-ups drank and danced the shag, I wandered along the moonlit bank until I found myself staring up at a neighbor's tree house. On a sagging platform that jutted out over the water, I sat watching the party, indistinct figures moving in the firelight. It had been maybe ten minutes when my mother noticed I was missing. After she checked the house, she stood at the end of the dock and called my name. There was real fear in her voice, and it sent a shiver through me. I climbed down and ran to her as fast as I could, calling out all the way, *I'm coming, I'm coming.*

•   •   •

When I was done with the vodka, I tossed the bottle into the lake, along with my grandfather's pills. By then it was late, almost ten, and the drizzle had turned to a downpour. I hardly noticed. On the way into town, I rolled down the windows and hit ninety miles an hour, the highway tightening around me like a tunnel as raindrops pelted the windshield. It's a miracle I made it to Lyle's.

"Where've you been?" he said, answering the door in his boxers.

"Nowhere." I wrung water from my shirt. "Out for a drive."

He fetched a towel while I slipped off my sandals and emptied the soggy contents of my pockets onto his kitchen counter. He was not happy about my going AWOL. He'd been calling the farm all day, and when nobody answered, he'd driven out to check on us. He found my grandfather sitting out front with a pitcher of bloody marys, waiting. He had his days mixed up; he thought it was Friday.

"That's my grandfather," I said. "Knows he wants a drink even if he doesn't know the day." I opened the refrigerator and helped myself to a beer as Lyle went on about how embarrassed Cal had been when he realized his mistake.

"I'm just glad he was okay," Lyle said. "I mean, at first I was almost afraid to go out there."

I had to roll my eyes at that. "If you're so afraid of him dying, why don't you get off your ass and do something?"

Lyle got up from the table and went into the bedroom to find some dry clothes. He was not going to fight with a drunk. "It's been a blast," I said, taking another swallow of beer and putting my sandals back on, but my keys were gone. Lyle had them, and he wouldn't give them back. "I don't think driving is a good idea," he said. When it finally

sank in that he was serious, I locked him out of the bedroom
and told him to sleep on the sofa. Then I lay in his bed, staring at the shadow of his feet beneath the door and waiting for
him to come get me. I wanted him to pick the lock, climb the
fire escape, kick down the door, stop at nothing. But he just
stood there knocking and asking me to open up, and eventually he went away. I heard him rummaging through the
closet, getting blankets and a pillow. I couldn't believe he
would give up so easily. I was sure he'd be back, but after a
few minutes, the light clicked off.

My mother loved water-skiing and swimming in the ocean
and horseback riding, but most of all she loved to race stock
cars. Before I was born, she was a two-time track champion
in the hobby division at Columbia Speedway, the only lady
driver among men who hated racing against a woman and
hated losing to one even more. Cal told me she'd always
liked driving fast, even before she got her license. Back then
he owned an old delivery truck he'd modified to haul silage.
In the fields along the edge of the swamp, he grew corn for
his cows. He'd cut the corn while it was still green and pack
it into a bunker silo, then cover it with a sheet of plastic until
it fermented, at which point he'd drain the runoff into silage
troughs that ran to the cattle lot at the back of the dairy
building.

But first the corn had to be hauled up to the silo, a job my
mother volunteered for as soon as she was able to reach the
truck's clutch. Even driving full-tilt with the windows down,
it was sweltering work, the piedmont sun beating down on
the cab until the steering wheel burned her fingers. One day
when the mercury hit 102, my mother decided she'd had

enough: she convinced a farmhand to help her take off the driver's-side door, claiming it was Cal's idea. They left it leaning against the milk house. My grandfather said it was a wonder she didn't kill herself that day, no seatbelt and no door, nothing but her grip on the wheel to keep her from flying into the air. The sight of her barreling like a madwoman up out of the swamp scared him so badly that he never let her drive the truck again. In fact, even after she got her license, he wouldn't let her drive the family Plymouth unless he was with her. My mother only made things worse when she borrowed the Plymouth and took her friends for a joyride that ended in a ditch along Bluff Road. Still, she would not be denied a car. As soon as she graduated from high school, she took a job in the parts department of the local Ford dealership, moved out, and bought herself an old convertible. Within a few years, she talked her boyfriend into getting her a race car, a '62 Fairlane, and began to make a name for herself at the track. Several times she invited Cal to come see her race, but she was still his little girl, and he could not bring himself to go.

The morning after I stole my grandfather's sleeping pills, I found my keys in Lyle's desk and snuck out while he was in the shower. Cal was already up when I got home. He came out of the bathroom holding his ivory-handled straight edge, his face half covered in shaving cream.

"You're bleeding," I said.

He dabbed his throat, smeared red between his fingers, winked at me. "Think a man could slit his own throat?"

I decided to hide the razor first chance I got—that, his shotgun shells, his hunting knife, whatever I could find. In the kitchen, I was getting a glass of tomato juice and some Tylenol when Cal appeared in galoshes, a fleck of tissue stuck to his Adam's apple. He said it was too wet for golf, that we should hunt arrowheads instead, and I agreed, thinking this might be our last time. The rain had finally stopped. Beyond the dairy building, the fog was just starting to lift, and the land smelled as rich as it had in my childhood, in the long-ago days when Cal used to spot arrowheads from high on the tractor as he dressed the fields. He'd taught me the best time to find them was after a storm, when the points gleamed white in the dark soil. We started at the barn and worked our way toward the bluff. Cal was in high spirits. He didn't mention Lyle's embarrassing visit the day before, nor did he comment on what poor shape I was in, wincing against the daylight, clinging to a thermos of coffee. Now that the house was done, he said, he wanted to celebrate by taking Lyle and me out to dinner.

"Ah," I said. "The Last Supper."

"Sure," he said. "We could do the lamb and leavened bread. But actually I was thinking fried shrimp and hush puppies at Captain's Calabash."

"Okay." I kept walking, wishing away the pain behind my eyes. We'd almost reached the bluff when he cleared his throat and asked me if, by the way, I wouldn't mind putting back his pills.

"I can't," I said. "I threw them in the lake."

He considered this as we turned and started back toward the barn. The sun had finally burned through the clouds, and wisps of steam were rising like ghosts from the wet earth. Behind us, at the edge of the swamp, crows cawed among the cypress and loblolly pines.

"You think I'm making a mistake," he said.

I held my breath and tried to focus on the muddy furrow at my feet. This was the first time he'd asked me point-blank what I thought. "I don't know," I said. "I just know I don't want you to do it."

Cal looked like he'd been expecting as much. He sighed a tired sigh and said he didn't want anybody having to take care of him. He'd been through all that with his father, and he wouldn't wish it on anyone.

"What if I *want* to take care of you?"

He knelt to pick up what looked to be a small quartz arrowhead, my question too ridiculous to answer, but as he wiped mud from the stone with his thumb, I kept after him, saying that I didn't see the hurry and that he should wait until he was truly sick, and besides, what ever happened to making the most of what you had left? Didn't he want to be with me as long as he could? He gave me a disapproving gaze, a look I imagine my mother saw a lot of.

"The only reason the Colonel didn't shoot his lights out is because he forgot to. That's not going to happen to me."

"Then why don't you let me help?" This was an idea that had been in the back of my mind for years, but until now I'd had the sense to keep it there. With a grunt, Cal hauled himself to his feet and sized me up, trying to decide if I really thought I was serious. At the moment, I suppose I did. "I could give you the pills myself," I said. "When the time comes."

This got him laughing, which turned into coughing, which reminded him of the crumpled pack of Winstons in his shirt pocket. He lit one up and played along. "And when would that be?"

I unscrewed the thermos and sipped lukewarm coffee. This question was, of course, the reason I'd always kept the

24

idea to myself, all the answers I could think of—when he could no longer remember his own name, no longer dress himself, no longer feed himself—being so arbitrary as to seem absurd, because how could I ever really know when his life was no longer worth living?

"You tell me," I said.

He couldn't help smiling at that, too, but it was a sad smile that didn't last—and I could see I was getting to him. After all those years wishing he'd done better by my mother, all those years trying not to make the same mistakes with me, now it came down to this: Would he or would he not abandon me? I understood that I was using his love for me like a crowbar, trying to pry a promise out of him by making one I'd never keep, but I couldn't stop myself. "Don't you care how I feel?"

"Of course I do." There was no longer irony in his voice, only resignation. He exhaled smoke, stared across the fields. "Okay. We'll do it your way."

"Okay?" I said. "You mean it?"

"What'd I just say?" He finished examining the stone and passed it to me with a shrug. It might have been a chipped spear point, or it might have just been a piece of quartz—neither of us could tell, but I put it in my pocket and carried it home.

Captain's Calabash was no five-star affair, but my grandfather was old-fashioned, and going out to dinner with him meant dressing up even if most of the other patrons were in jeans. He wore his favorite seersucker suit, and I wore a blue cocktail dress I'd bought for rush. On the answering-machine message Cal left for Lyle, he advised him to look sharp as well, but Lyle didn't call back. He didn't return my call, either, the breathless message I'd left telling him about Cal's change of heart. That surprised me—I figured he'd race over as soon as he got the news—but I wasn't going to let Lyle's absence spoil our dinner.

My grandfather was another story. "What's keeping Lyle?" he said, checking his watch. "Think he got my call?" We were sitting in a corner booth beneath a mounted swordfish, picking at an appetizer plate of steamed clams. So far, the evening didn't feel like much of a celebration. Cal had shown little interest in anything except his wine. All day, I'd been trying to cheer him up. I wanted to believe I hadn't talked him into anything, that in the end, he was just like anyone else, in no hurry to die; I wanted to believe he was no more able to let go of me than I was of him. "You and Lyle," he said, "you aren't fighting?" I refilled his glass and tried to change the subject, talking about things we might do now that the house was finished. Cal just nodded along as I suggested a week at the beach, a trip to California to see his sister. It wasn't until Lyle rolled into the restaurant at six-thirty, full of apologies, that Cal finally perked up. Lyle explained he'd been out shopping for a suit, then hustled around town looking for a tailor who could do alterations on the spot.

"Didn't find one," he said, wiggling his arms inside the long sleeves of his jacket.

"You look fine," Cal said.

"For a circus clown," I added, but Lyle was in too good a mood to take offense. You could tell a weight had been lifted from his shoulders: The end of his work hadn't meant the end of Cal after all. Once we placed our orders, Cal excused himself to go to the bathroom. Lyle turned to me.

"Well?"

I feigned interest in the swordfish. "I guess he realized he was being selfish. Not that you'd ever have told him so."

"So the stranger who showed up at my apartment last night," Lyle said, "she's still with us?"

"You should wash your sheets," I said. "They still smell like turpentine. And you shouldn't have let me sleep alone."

He picked up a cocktail napkin and waved it like a white flag. "Ten-four. Won't happen again."

I wasn't going to let him off so easily, but he looked like he meant it, and when Cal came out of the bathroom and smiled at the sight of us together, I couldn't stay mad. The night turned into a celebration after all. We ended up with more food than three people could possibly eat—baskets of hush puppies and popcorn shrimp, platters of broiled oysters, scallops, flounder. Cal was in top form, ordering a bottle of champagne and flirting with the waitresses even more than usual. He brought up my idea of spending a week at the beach and declared that all three of us should go. "I've got a friend with a house at Surfside," he said. "We'll rent a boat, do some crabbing." Watching him preside over the table, seeing him in such an expansive mood, I knew I'd done the right thing. We'd still have months together, maybe years.

After dinner, Lyle followed us back to the farm for a nightcap, at which time Cal suggested a round of golf in the morning. We'd play at Forest Acres, then have lunch in the clubhouse. I told him I wasn't ready to play in front of other people, but he just clinked his brandy glass against mine and told me to follow his lead. "Remember," he said, "you can observe a lot just by watching."

•　　•　　•

27

Shortly after I came to live with my grandfather, I decided to join my mother in heaven. My father had been gone for weeks, and though I'd not yet given up on him, I wanted to punish him for leaving me, and I wanted to punish my grandfather for thinking he could take my parents' place. With half a peanut butter sandwich in my shirt pocket, I climbed out the dormer window of my bedroom and onto the roof. Below me, the propane tank glowed dull in the moonlight, a soft patter of raindrops on its metallic surface. My plan was to jump, but after I stood there awhile, gauging the distance between me and the ground, I decided to run away to heaven instead. From the corner of the roof, I was able to reach the chinaberry tree, but as I shimmied past Cal's window, the branches scraped glass. By the time I reached the wet grass he was there, smoking a cigarette and looking at me like I was a mule. He took my hand and led me back inside, where he toweled my hair, helped me into dry pajamas, and tucked me into bed. On his way out, he stopped at the door. "Look here," he said. "If you want to run away, I'm not going to stop you. I'm getting too old for that." Then he shut off the light.

But the next morning, in spite of himself, he was up at the crack of dawn with his tools. He nailed my screen shut, pruned the chinaberry tree so that its branches no longer reached the roof, and installed deadbolt locks on the doors. For weeks, he slept with the keys on a string around his neck, and unlike my mother, who in my place probably would have stolen them while he slept, I was comforted by the thought that he wanted to keep me close, that I was too precious to be let go.

• • •

After we finished our brandy, Lyle and I went back to his apartment and got busy making up for the previous night. We ended up oversleeping and had to hurry to the farm the next morning, when we were supposed to meet Cal. As soon as we turned off Bluff Road, I knew something wasn't right. The newspaper was still in the yard, the porch light still on. Inside, the house was silent, save the ticking of the cuckoo clock on the mantel.

We called an ambulance, but it was too late. Cal sat slumped in his recliner, an empty pill bottle and rock glass on the table beside him. He still had his suit on, and as he sat there, motionless, it seemed as if the wide lapels were pressing down, pinning him against the worn upholstery. He did not look peaceful so much as deflated, his lips parted where the air had left him.

While Lyle was talking to 911, I held Cal's hand like I should have done when he died—like he would have wanted me to, though of course he'd never have asked. I was crying so hard and so loud that Lyle had to take the phone into the bathroom. It was bad enough that Cal was gone, but to think he'd died alone because of me, because I'd left him no choice but to go behind my back, that was almost more than I could take. My tears were making a spotty mess of his trousers. His skin was already cold, his fingers stiff. I would learn later that he'd been dead for hours, that he'd probably taken the pills as soon as we left.

When Lyle got off the phone, he came back into the den and put his arms around me. In between sobs, I tried to make him understand this was all my fault, but he kept insisting I wasn't to blame, that regardless of what I'd said or done, things had turned out more or less the way Cal planned—he'd simply done what he thought was best, and we had to accept that. I knew Lyle was right, but even so, it would be a long time before I could forgive any of us. He was still holding me when the medics arrived, sirens splitting the morning air. "Careful," he said, gently prying my fingers loose from Cal's. "You don't want to bruise him."

CHAPTER TWO

1971

Wylie

Around the time Wylie Greer's daughter was born, he had the bad luck to get mixed up with a man he knew—a brand-new father like himself—who got drunk one night and accidentally killed his infant son. The man's name was Lester Hardin, and on Thursday nights he raced his old Ford in the hobby division out at Columbia Speedway, same as Maddy used to. Lester kept to himself in the pit area and never had two words for Maddy and Wylie, but there was nothing in particular about him to make you think he'd hurt his own son. He was just another gearhead who hated racing against a woman and no doubt wished Maddy good riddance when she got pregnant and quit.

It wasn't until Lester heard Maddy was selling the Fairlane that he tried getting friendly with them. One night in the summer of 1971, he buddied up to Wylie in the infield to inquire about the car. This was a few months after Wylie and Maddy had moved into a clapboard cottage on her father's dairy farm, trying to save for the baby. At the time Wylie was working as a mechanic at the Ford dealership, but on Thursday nights he'd been moonlighting at the track, picking up a few extra bucks clearing wrecks for an outfit called Atlas

Towing. Mostly the job was an excuse to watch the races now that Maddy wasn't driving anymore—that and a chance to talk up the Fairlane to the other drivers. After all the blood and sweat he'd poured into that car, after all the races he and Maddy had won, he hated the thought of selling it, but they needed the cash.

Wylie didn't resent Maddy or the baby or even the prospect of fatherhood in general, though it was true, here in the homestretch, that he'd started second-guessing himself. Every time Maddy grabbed his hand and held it to her stomach (and she did this constantly) he was more convinced that he didn't have what it took, that he lacked the enthusiasm or patience for kids—in short, that he'd make a half-assed father, no better than his own, the kind of man who ends up ruining his family or leaving it.

When Lester ambled over, Maddy was holed up inside the wrecker reading Dr. Spock while Wylie watched the late models take practice laps. Lester offered him a beer from the six-pack dangling on his finger, then tapped his can against Wylie's.

"To fatherhood," he said. "To babies that sleep all night and look like their daddies."

Lester's wife, Gladys, was pregnant, too, eight months to Maddy's six, but Wylie didn't feel like talking babies with a guy who acted as though they were just another notch on his belt. In fact, he didn't much feel like talking babies at all. When Lester started telling him about the fancy cigars he'd bought for the big day, Wylie tuned him out and found himself staring at the wrecker's door, the hand-painted silhouette of Atlas straining under the weight of the globe.

By the time Lester finally got around to asking about the car, Gladys had started back from the concession stand with a milkshake, picking her way through the muddy infield. She had the glazed-over look in her eyes that Maddy was starting to get—like she was so deep in her own private babyland that any minute she might wander off or float away—but the second the mothers-to-be recognized each other, they both clicked into focus. Maddy hauled herself out of the truck, the two of them suddenly carrying on like long-lost sisters, though before that night they'd been nothing more than casual friends. After a minute or so, Lester horned in, trying to make nice with Maddy. He pointed at her stomach and asked her did she have a little Richard Petty in there.

"It's a girl," Maddy said, an idea she'd been clinging to since the day she learned she was pregnant.

"Ah." Lester crushed his beer can and tossed it in the grass. "Future race queen."

Maddy stood there with her arms crossed, staring Lester down until he understood he'd put his foot in his mouth.

"Louise Smith, then!" he said. "Ethel Flock!" These were old-time lady drivers, a couple of Maddy's heroes. She let him off the hook with a thin smile and turned back to Gladys, leaving Wylie and Lester to talk money.

Lester wanted the Fairlane at half the asking price. Wylie almost told him where to stick it, but no one else was interested and Maddy's due date was coming up fast; half was better than nothing at all. At the end of the night, worn down by Lester's haggling, Wylie finally caved. They shook on it, Lester said he'd call as soon as he got the cash together, and that was the last Wylie heard from him.

Over the next few weeks, though, their wives were on the phone almost every day, and before long it wasn't just the

35

details of Maddy's pregnancy that crowded out all other topics of conversation between her and Wylie—now he had to make room in his head for Gladys's pregnancy, too. Maddy had gained x pounds so far; Gladys was up to y. Maddy had terrible leg cramps. Gladys had terrible gas. Neither of them believed in pacifiers. Both of them were going to breast-feed. Early on, Wylie had been willing—even eager—to listen, but the more he'd learned about babies, the more he realized he'd never know all that was required, and after a while, he'd simply given up.

When Nat was born, Maddy visited Gladys in the hospital, and afterward she kept Gladys company and helped out with the baby over at the Hardins' place. Wylie got regular reports on Nat—what thick brown hair he had, what a bruiser he was, how much he drooled. Occasionally Wylie also got word through his wife that Lester was having trouble coming up with the money for the Fairlane, that Gladys was on his case for even thinking about buying it, but now that she and Gladys were so close, Maddy didn't want to get involved.

Then one night, when Nat was about two months old, Gladys came home from work to discover him facedown in his crib. The deputy coroner ruled it an accidental suffocation. Wylie heard about Nat before Maddy did, from a guy in parts who'd stopped by the car wash that Lester managed over on Rosewood Drive. Wylie left the dealership early, drove straight home in a steady rain. Maddy was already two days overdue, gingerly pacing the house, and he wanted to give her the news himself, rather than have her hear it from a hysterical Gladys. When he told her, she dropped the ladle she'd been stirring the chili with and walked out of the kitchen. He found her in the bathroom on the edge of the tub, poking at her stomach, and when she looked up at him, her look said, *Promise it'll be okay,* but also, *You can't make it okay, and if it's not, I'll always blame you.*

"She's been kicking all day," she said. "Now she won't move."

Wylie put his arm around his wife and told her that what had happened to Lester and Gladys wasn't going to happen to them. He told her, as they sat there listening to the rain and waiting for the baby to kick, that Lester and Gladys's loss tilted the odds in their favor.

Five days later, Wylie was standing in a recovery room at Richland Memorial with his mother and father-in-law, holding his daughter for the first time. "We are so lucky," Maddy said. "Do you have any idea how lucky we are?" She was propped up in bed, bleary-eyed and red-faced from thirteen hours of labor, but happy—crying with happiness and relief, and gazing at her husband and daughter as if the world started and ended right there. She'd never seemed to doubt that Wylie was cut out for kids, and so he'd been living off her faith in him as if it were his own, although he was sure that faith had less to do with him than with how badly she wanted a baby. Now, as she sat there beaming, he clucked his tongue at Holly and waited to feel something besides scared. He had hoped for what Maddy was feeling—love at first sight, love washing over him like a wave. But here he was, just holding a baby. It could have been anybody's baby. His mother and Cal kept saying she was the prettiest little thing, and she did have pretty lips, but her hands looked too big for her body, and she seemed so feeble, so raw. He took a seat on the bed and played This Little Piggy with her toes, telling himself to give it some time.

Later, after the parents left and the nurse had taken Holly away, Wylie went down to the cafeteria. On his way back, he stopped at the nursery. Looking through the window at the row of babies, he doubted he'd be able to tell which one was Holly, but there she was, staring off into space like a little insomniac, as if she already had a head full of worries. He tapped on the glass and waved, trying to get her attention.

When he got back to the room, Maddy was still awake, sitting up in bed and looking out the door. "I think that's the room Gladys had," she said. "Right across the hall." She leaned back, moved her dinner tray so Wylie would have a place to sit. "Do you think I'm a terrible friend?"

It had been five days since Nat died, and Maddy still hadn't spoken to Gladys. This was during the time when everyone still believed Nat's death had been a natural one, before Lester confessed. Out at the track, the hobby drivers had held a charity race to help pay for the funeral, but Maddy had stayed home. She'd skipped the funeral, too. She'd even stopped answering the phone, afraid it might be Gladys.

Wylie kissed Maddy's neck. She tasted salty, like she used to after a race. "You haven't heard from her, either."

"But I should have been at the funeral. I didn't even send flowers."

"Then call her," he said. "She'll understand."

Maddy sighed. "The thing is, I don't want to."

Maddy had wanted Wylie to take a week off work when the baby was born, but without the money from the Fairlane, all he could manage was a couple of days. His mother and Cal were eager to help out with Holly, but Maddy

38

wanted to feel like she was in control before she let the grandparents swoop in, and from the looks of it, that wasn't about to happen anytime soon. It was amazing, really, how quickly things went to hell. Holly cried and cried and wouldn't stop. Crying wasn't even the word for it. Screaming, shrieking, wailing, she worked herself into a frenzy. The only thing that shut her up was Maddy's breast, and she wanted it constantly—every two hours, every hour. Wylie and Maddy never slept. She accused him of sulking; he accused her of spoiling the baby. In no time, they were on the brink of hating each other, and Wylie felt the weight of it bearing down on him, despair like nothing he'd ever known.

On the third morning, before work, Wylie slipped out of the house during one of Holly's meltdowns, telling Maddy he needed to give the Fairlane a tune-up. She followed him to the door with the crying baby.

"That's it," she said. "Just run off and hide. Like father, like son."

Wylie stopped halfway across the yard, made himself breathe. "Fine, honey. You do the car, I'll watch the baby."

"You wouldn't know where to start," Maddy said, letting the screen door slam shut.

Wylie had finally gotten around to running an ad in the paper once he realized Lester couldn't afford the car, but in the whirlwind leading up to Holly's arrival, he'd let the ad lapse, and the car had been parked at the end of the lane ever since, a FOR SALE sign fading in the windshield. He swapped out the spark plugs and was almost done changing the oil when he looked up to see Maddy coming down the gravel lane, stone-faced and barefoot, Holly asleep in her arms. She patted the car's fender. "I've come to say my good-byes," she said.

For three years, that car had been their life, and during the early months of Maddy's pregnancy, it stung Wylie to think of the summers they'd spent in the hobby division, how their climb up the NASCAR ladder was finished before they'd reached the second rung. But eventually he bought into the idea that a baby could be better than racing, that a baby could bring him and Maddy closer together.

He asked Maddy if she wanted to take the car for a spin, and she said no, she just wanted to sit in it for a while. As soon as she settled in behind the wheel, Holly woke, hungry again. The baby was so frantic she had trouble latching on to Maddy's nipple. Normally Wylie would have helped, parting Holly's lips the way the nurse had done, but his hands were slick with motor oil, so he waited until Maddy had things under control, then lowered the hood and gave her a thumbs-up, just like he used to do before each race. Maddy was focused on the baby, though, and with the morning dew still streaking the windshield, she didn't even seem to see him.

In between fitful meals, Holly continued to wail, so after Wylie got off work they took her to the doctor. The doctor told them she was fine. Maddy despised him for saying so—"Nat's doctor said he was fine, too"—and Wylie despised her for despising him. The night before, she'd ventured that maybe Holly's crying was God's way of punishing her for abandoning Gladys. This from a woman who hadn't set foot in a church since she was confirmed. Wylie didn't think God had anything to do with it; the problem had to be that Holly wasn't getting enough to eat. Something was wrong with Maddy's milk, or there just wasn't enough of it. Otherwise, why was Holly always hungry? But the doctor told them her weight was right on target. "If you're still worried," he said, "you can always try formula." Maddy sneered at this, too. If God wanted babies to drink formula, she told Wylie, she'd have tin cans for tits.

That night, after Holly's midnight meal, Wylie drifted off into a hazy twilight between waking and sleeping and then rolled over to find himself alone in bed. A light was on in the kitchen. Maddy stood at the counter in her nightshirt, paging through a cookbook and marshaling ingredients: eggs, flour, a bottle of vanilla extract.

"What are you doing?"

"Making Gladys a pound cake," she said.

"It's one in the morning."

She cracked an egg and dropped the shell into the garbage. "Then go back to bed." She wouldn't even look at him.

Twenty minutes later, Holly started crying. He got up and changed her diaper—the only one of her problems he knew how to fix. When he was done, he brought her to Maddy.

"I think she's hungry again."

"The kitchen is closed," Maddy said. "I just fed her an hour ago." She was sitting at the table, looking like she'd had about all she could take. There was flour everywhere.

"If we got some formula," Wylie said, rocking Holly against his shoulder, "I could give her a bottle while you slept."

Maddy sighed, as if the very sight of him wore her out. "How many times do I have to tell you? There's a *reason* milk is coming out of me." She got up from the table and took a few bills from the coffee can on top of the refrigerator. She told Wylie to go to the bakery in the morning, buy a pound cake, and deliver it to Gladys. "Try to get one that looks homemade." She rummaged under the counter. "Put it in this."

Wylie stared at the Tupperware container she was holding. "You're kidding, right?" Going to see Lester and Gladys was the last thing he wanted to do. He was sorry Maddy felt bad, but he was tired, and they weren't his friends, and frankly he didn't want to face them any more than she did. The whole business with the Fairlane just made things that much worse. Though he didn't appreciate Lester stringing him along, wasting his time, he didn't want to show up on the guy's doorstep and make him feel like he had to apologize—not at a time like this.

"Go ahead and get a card, too," Maddy said. "Sign my name. But don't be gone long. I can't do everything here."

Wylie took the container and held it up for Holly to touch. He was determined not to raise his voice. "Honey," he said, "if you want to give Gladys a cake, take it over there yourself."

Lester and Gladys lived in a neighborhood of small brick duplexes in West Columbia, about a mile from the track. Wylie found their place easily enough, but he didn't know what he was going to say to them, so he kept driving, aimless, hoping their rusty Dart would be gone by the time he came back. He ended up out by the track and turned off into the rutted meadow that doubled as a parking lot. It was Thursday, and he was due back there that night; he'd called in sick at the dealership, but he hadn't been able to find anyone at Atlas to cover his shift at the track. He wished he could curl up in his car and sleep until then. The gate on the front stretch was wide open, and inside he could see the owner, Sid Gooden, slowly working his way around the banked oval atop his state-surplus motor grader, pushing the clay and sand back toward the bottom of the track.

The summer before, Maddy had been leading a qualifying heat when she fishtailed and hit the guardrail, which wasn't much of a rail at all, just sheets of plywood nailed to a fence. As she sat there crosswise on the track, stalled out and waiting for the red flag, the rest of the pack came sliding through the turn. You could hear the whole infield suck in its breath, bracing for a crash. Wylie always told himself that Maddy was invincible out there—he couldn't afford to think about it any other way—but seeing her come so close to getting T-boned rattled him. When she got back to the pit area, he asked her to sit out the feature race so he could look over the car. He didn't think she'd go for it—she'd been in wrecks before, had shrugged them off and hopped back in the saddle—but that night, after she finished cursing her luck and loose dirt, she allowed that maybe it wasn't a bad idea.

The following Sunday, he took her over to Darlington and dropped half a paycheck on good seats for the Southern 500, the race Maddy dreamed of running. He was thinking it'd be just the thing to help them shake off the cobwebs, but Maddy spent most of the race staring at the pregnant girl next to them—was so busy staring, in fact, that she missed Buddy Baker's Dodge crossing the finish line. Wylie was lowering his binoculars when she hooked an arm around his waist and shouted into his ear. "Let's! Have! A baby!"

At first he thought she was joking, making fun of the pregnant girl for the way she'd been rubbing her stomach all afternoon. Anyhow, the plan had always been that they'd try for a baby after they quit racing, a day Wylie figured was a long ways off. But Maddy was in his ear again, ahead of him as usual, telling him she was afraid she might not be around to *have* a baby if she kept racing.

Now, as he watched Sid take another turn on his grader, smoothing out the grooves, Wylie thought of the two hobby titles Maddy had won, how good he'd felt knowing she couldn't do it without him and that he'd never let her down. That's how he felt that afternoon at Darlington when he said yes to having a baby. It was the last time he'd felt that way.

Gladys answered the door. It was almost lunchtime, but she was still in her bathrobe, squinting at Wylie through the torn screen as if she hadn't seen sunlight in days, a road map of red in her eyes. When she noticed the cake, she invited him in like she didn't have a choice.

"Lester," she called, "friend of yours."

The curtains were drawn in the narrow living room, and except for the traffic out on 321, the house was quiet. Wylie hadn't expected Lester to be home. He hadn't even meant to come in. He'd hoped to hand off the cake at the front door and be gone. Now he tried for a sympathetic smile and told Gladys how sorry Maddy was that she couldn't come herself. "She had the baby on Sunday," he said.

"Please tell her I've been meaning to stop by," Gladys said, but it didn't sound like she meant it. It sounded like she just wanted to be left alone. She stood there cinching her robe until Lester came out of the kitchen. When he shook Wylie's hand, he clasped it with both of his, the way a preacher does. Wylie told them he and Maddy had been praying for them ever since they heard about Nat. "We're deeply sorry for your loss," he said. This was something he'd rehearsed in the truck, and to his ears, that's how it sounded.

"You're a good guy to come all the way out here," Lester said. "I just put on some coffee. Let's sit down and have some of that—what do you got there?"

"Maddy's pound cake."

"Gladys loves pound cake, don't you, hon?" He put an arm around his wife, but she shrugged him off.

"I'm not hungry," she said, and then she went into the bedroom and shut the door. Lester looked embarrassed. He rubbed a hand back and forth across his crew cut. Wylie was about to say he should be getting home when Lester cleared his throat.

"I keep telling her we can try again," he said, shaking his head. "She don't want to hear it." He glanced at the bedroom door, then held up the cake as if to say, *But there's this.* Wylie followed him into the kitchen and sat at the dinette while Lester cut two slices. "You know, it could have been a lot worse," Lester said, lowering his voice. "I mean, Christ, the kid was only eight weeks old. It's not like we had much time to get attached to him." He set a cup of coffee in front of Wylie. "Right? You must know what I mean."

Wylie supposed he did. If something terrible was going to happen to your baby, better sooner than later, before she started trusting you to make everything okay. Still, as soon as he nodded, it felt like a betrayal. Pretty soon he'd be telling Lester he wasn't sure why he'd wanted a baby in the first place. "Me and Maddy," he said, "we just feel so lucky—"

Lester cut him off. "Goes without saying." His smile was tight. He took a bite of cake and Wylie got to work on his, too, promising himself he'd get out of there as soon as he was done. He was almost finished when Lester lit a cigarette

and warmed up to him again, apologizing about the Fairlane.
Wylie told him it was no big deal, but Lester went on and on,
saying he'd never meant to leave Wylie in the lurch. Things
had gotten so busy with the baby, he said, and money was
tight. He still wanted to buy the car, though, assuming Wylie
hadn't already sold it.

"Not yet," Wylie said.

Lester slid the pack of smokes across the table, said that
originally the car was going to be a present for himself, to
celebrate the baby, but now he wanted it as a surprise for
Gladys. He said that since she started hanging around
Maddy more, she'd been talking about entering a powder-
puff derby—not *racing* racing, just girls versus girls—and
although he'd been against it at first, now he thought it
might do her some good. Wylie shook a cigarette from the
pack and nodded along. He didn't believe Lester would end
up buying the car any more than he believed Gladys would
want it, but he decided to give Lester the benefit of the
doubt and told him he'd hold off renewing the ad, give
them time to work something out.

"In that case," Lester said, "why don't I come get the car
today?" He said he could swing by the bank, bring Wylie a
deposit that afternoon, and pay him the rest next week.
Wylie tapped the end of his cigarette on the table. This
wasn't at all what he'd had in mind, but he was in too deep
to back out now, and he was too tired to argue. He hadn't
slept in four days, his wife would sooner growl at him than
smile, and he was starting to think he'd rather sit there
smoking with Lester than go home and face his own kid's
howling. He took one last gulp of coffee and stood to leave.

"Deal."

• • •

On the way home, Wylie fell asleep at the wheel and drifted off the road, his tires biting into the grassy shoulder. A row of scrub pines floated before him. He jerked upright and wrestled the car onto the blacktop, cursing Maddy for sending him to see Gladys, cursing himself for giving in to Lester again. Shaken, he stopped at a convenience store for another cup of coffee and—debating whether to buy it even as he approached the register—a can of formula. Just in case Maddy changes her mind, he told himself. When he got home, she was asleep in bed with Holly. The baby stirred as he looked in on them, and before he had time to think twice, he whisked her out of the room. He knew you were supposed to heat the formula, but he was afraid Maddy would wake up, so he told Holly she'd have to drink it cold. He sat at the dining room table with her in the crook of his arm like a football, brushing the nipple against her cheek the way he'd seen Maddy do, dribbling formula onto her lips. She turned her head from side to side, trying to get away from it. "Come on, cupcake," he said. "Let's be reasonable." She began to fuss, and when he persisted, sweating and shaking, she started to cry in earnest. He had to remind himself that she wasn't doing it on purpose; she was only a baby. She needed to eat, whether she wanted to or not, and he didn't know when he'd get another chance. Finally, he worked the nipple between her lips, and when she tried to spit it out, he held firm, determined that she'd at least have a taste, no matter how much she fought and flailed her little arms. It wasn't until she began to choke that he finally eased up. As he pulled the bottle away, she coughed formula onto his arm and shrieked, a sound as terrible as a loose fan belt. "Now, now," he said, "there, there," but she went on and on, screaming bloody murder. It was all he could do not to shove the bottle back into her mouth, just to shut her up.

Somehow Maddy slept through the whole thing, and Wylie spent the next hour trying to make it up to Holly, carrying her around the house and singing nursery rhymes while he waited for Lester. Once she stopped crying, she didn't seem to hold a grudge. It was as if Sid had come along with his grader, smoothing out all the ruts between them.

Lester never showed up with the money, and he wasn't at the races that night, either. Same old, same old, Wylie thought. He'd been a half hour late getting to the track himself and, despite three large Cokes, nodded off in the wrecker. A track steward had to tap on the window to wake him when one of the drivers blew a tire.

Back home, it was business as usual—distraught wife, crying baby. This time Wylie suggested they get out for a walk. The night was warm and breezy, and they followed the dirt lane past the soybean field, past the farmhouse where Cal had been cooling his heels until Maddy lifted her restraining order. Holly was asleep on Wylie's shoulder within minutes.

"Look at you," Maddy said. "You're a natural." For the first time all day, she seemed relaxed. She slipped her hand in his, swung her arm as they walked. Wylie stroked Holly's head and glanced up at the stars. *This* was how he'd always imagined life with a baby, he and Maddy exhausted but not defeated, pulling together.

They were nearing the end of the lane when they heard the crash. At first Wylie thought somebody had hit a deer, but then there was another crash, and another. As they got closer to the highway, he could see in the moonlight a figure standing on the hood of the Fairlane, stomping the windshield. He wanted it to be some local kid, Bluff Road riffraff, but he recognized the Dart idling on the roadside. After one last stomp, Lester hopped down and grabbed what looked to be a crowbar from his backseat. Wylie tried to pass the baby to Maddy, but she held on to his arm.

"Don't," she whispered. "He's drunk off his ass."

And then Lester began to whale on the Fairlane's fender. The first blow woke Holly, but Lester didn't hear her crying until he'd taken three or four more swings. Turning, he peered through the darkness, the crowbar cocked in his hand. Wylie took a step toward him.

"All right, Lester," he called. "Better get on home now."

For a moment Lester stood and stared, his shoulders heaving with each breath. Holly continued to howl. In the distance, headlights appeared, the rumble of a tractor trailer. Finally Lester reared back and flung the crowbar into the underbrush across the road. The Dart sprayed a rooster tail of gravel as he pulled away.

When his taillights faded, Wylie and Maddy walked over for a look at the Fairlane, saw what a number he'd done—all four tires knifed, the driver's seat shredded down to foam and springs, the windshield intact but caved in. Wylie picked up the FOR SALE sign, brushed it off, tossed it onto the seat. Once upon a time, he'd poured his heart and soul into that car. Now all he cared about, really, was how he'd get Lester to pay for the damage.

"Guess he changed his mind about the car," Wylie said.

Maddy just shook her head like she'd been expecting this all along. Wylie thought she'd be more upset, but he saw then that she'd let go, too, that whatever happened to the Fairlane now didn't much matter to her.

The next morning, when Wylie called the police, the dispatcher asked him to repeat Lester's name, said wait a minute, then came back on the line and informed him that Lester Hardin was already in custody. She asked Wylie to come down to the station to file his report. When he got there, he was greeted by a detective, an older man with puffy eyes and a dark suit that looked slept in. They knew each other from the dealership: the detective brought in his '68 Fastback GT for an oil change every two thousand miles on the nose. His office was as tidy as his car, a small, bright room with photos of his wife and daughter arranged on the windowsill. He pulled up a seat for Wylie. When Wylie asked what Lester was doing in jail, the detective took off his glasses, rubbed his eyes, and told him.

Shortly after he'd finished with Maddy's car, Lester had walked into the Richland County sheriff's office and confessed to the first officer he saw, a young deputy at the front desk. Lester told him about the night he'd been home alone with Nat while Gladys was waiting tables at the Waffle House. They'd been having their usual fight before she left, and he was sick of hearing her complain about money, about his job at the car wash, about having to leave her baby four nights a week just so they could make ends meet. Lester spent the evening in front of the TV with a bottle of whiskey, listening to the baby cry and trying to decide what to do about his life. When he'd had enough of the noise, he went into the nursery and held Nat, muffling the baby's cries against his chest. All he was trying to do, he told the deputy, was shut Nat up, get him to go to sleep. But the harder the baby cried, the harder Lester held him, and by the time he let go, Nat wasn't breathing. Lester then placed him facedown in the crib, and that's how Gladys found her baby when she got home. When he was done talking, Lester begged the deputy to shoot him.

At first, Wylie couldn't quite get his head around what he was hearing. It was so horrible, he thought Lester must have made it up. What was worse, every time he tried to make it real, every time he tried to picture Lester smothering his baby, what he saw instead was himself cramming that bottle into Holly's mouth. The two events ran together like water in his mind. For a moment *he* had an impulse to confess, if for no other reason than to hear the detective tell him he'd done nothing wrong. He sat quietly while the detective finished the story. He was saying that Lester finally confessed to Gladys last night, had actually gotten down on his knees and pleaded for forgiveness, at which point she'd told him she wished he were dead.

"Then she gave him a choice," the detective said. "Turn himself in, or she'd do it for him."

Wylie sat up straight, heard himself asking if Lester meant to kill the baby. The detective shrugged. "He says he didn't. Says it was an accident. We're just trying to find out what we can, which is why I wanted to hear about last night." He pulled out a notepad and began asking questions about what happened with Lester and the Fairlane. Wylie had trouble concentrating. He had to force himself to make eye contact with the detective. Starting with the night Lester approached him at the track, he told everything he could remember, hoping he'd say something that would be of use. The anger he was feeling toward Lester went beyond what

he'd done to the Fairlane, beyond Nat's death even. A half
hour later, as Wylie walked out of the station and into the
morning glare, he wished the policeman had honored
Lester's request and shot him on the spot.

Wylie had been planning to swing by Atlas and borrow a
flatbed, then haul the Fairlane out to a buddy's junkyard in
Irmo and sell it for parts, take whatever they'd give him.
Now that seemed like more than he could manage. He
stopped for a six-pack and pointed his car home, gunning
the engine past the juke joints and matchbox houses along
Bluff Road, slowing down only to look at the ruined shell of
the Fairlane as he turned off the highway. Halfway between
the farmhouse and the cottage, he pulled over and switched
off the ignition, sat there drinking and staring across the field
at the cows. One beer, two beers, three. He told himself he
was working up the courage to tell Maddy about Lester,
but mostly he was thinking about his father: his brooding,
his shouting, the whistle of his belt. It occurred to Wylie that
maybe his father had done him a favor, that maybe he'd left
to keep from doing more harm.

After the fourth beer, Wylie slid the bottles under his
seat and drove the rest of the way home. Maddy was out
front with Holly and a fistful of Kleenex, sitting on the
porch swing where she and Wylie used to spend evenings
watching the sun set behind Cal's silos. She looked like she
was done for. At first Wylie thought she'd already heard
about Lester, but it wasn't that—just another morning of
trying and failing to please Holly. He was barely out of the
truck when Maddy thrust the baby into his arms.

"You take her," she said. She blew her nose and began

telling him about Holly's latest fit, how she'd tried feeding her on one side and then the other, but nothing was good enough. "She's not even a week old and she already hates me." Maddy was so worked up, she didn't ask Wylie about his visit to the police station until they were inside. When he told her about Lester, she covered her mouth, shook her head as if it weren't true. "Poor Nat!" she said. "Poor Nat! Poor little baby!" That got Holly going again, and if it hadn't been for the four beers cushioning him from all the crying and misery, Wylie thought he might have started bawling himself.

Later, though, when Maddy had gotten past the shock of it, she told him she was actually relieved. "When it was a baby dying in his sleep, that was even worse," she said. "That could happen to anyone."

They were sitting on the floor with Holly between them on a blanket. Wylie lifted her up and blew a raspberry on her stomach but stopped when he noticed Maddy watching him. He thought she was about to accuse him of smelling like beer. "You know, if it weren't for you," she said, "he might never have confessed. Seeing you must have done it, made him realize what he'd done. Otherwise, why would he bust up our car on his way to the police?"

Wylie stood and carried Holly to the window. He thought about the Fairlane, imagined Lester plunging a knife into its tires, stomping the windshield. He had to admit, he liked the idea of being the one who'd pushed him over the edge. He liked the idea of Lester wishing he were in his shoes. But for all he knew, the only things separating him from Lester were circumstance and a little luck, and he was surprised Maddy didn't see it this way, too.

Maddy got up and went into the bathroom, asked Wylie from behind the door to check Holly's diaper. The toilet flushed, and then she said, "What I don't get is, how could Gladys not have known? She lived with the guy. She was married to him." Wylie unpinned Holly's diaper, saw that it was clean, and refastened it. When Maddy turned on the faucet, he picked up a small blue pillow from the rocking chair. Holly was kicking as he held it above her face. He tried to imagine lowering the pillow, pressing down, but he couldn't do it, not even for a second—as if that proved anything. But who was to say? Maybe Maddy was right. Maybe she saw something in Wylie he couldn't yet see in himself. He pulled the pillow away and whispered, "Peekaboo," trying to make a game of it. He figured Holly would start crying then, but she just lay there, blinking. That was what really got him: she didn't even have the sense to be afraid.

"Not that I blame Gladys," Maddy was saying. "Besides, she really needs me now. I was thinking I'd go see her tomorrow, if you'd drive me over." She shut off the water. "Are you listening?"

Wylie leaned over and kissed Holly on the tip of her nose. When he stood up, the room spun a little. He had time to set the pillow aside as Maddy came out of the bathroom, but he kept on holding it, and then he felt her behind him in the doorway, probably leaning there with her arms crossed, wondering why he was standing over their baby with a pillow. "I'm listening," he said.

CHAPTER THREE

1991

Lyle

Holly thinks she can drive as fast as she wants without get-ting busted. The secret, she says, is whiskey. Drinking lets her believe she's invisible, ergo, she is. "Two cops on the median and me doing ninety," she told me after the first time she ran off. "They nailed the guy in front of me *and* the guy behind me."

That's the story I couldn't get out of my head when she went AWOL again. I figured the next time I saw her, she'd be behind bars, or in the hospital, or laid out on a steel table. But somehow, after three days on the road, she makes it back to my apartment in one piece. It's a Saturday morn-ing, early November, and she's knocking softly at my door, like she doesn't want to wake me but if she has to, she will. At first I just lie there on the sofa, making her wait, making her sweat a little of what I've been sweating. She's supposed to be deciding whether she'll marry me—I asked her a month ago—but instead she's been off looking for her father again. Suddenly, after years of *to hell with him,* finding Wylie is the most important thing in the world—more important than school, more important than the farm, more important than us.

When I open the door, she sinks into me, holding on for dear life, and even though I'd like to wring her neck for running off without so much as a good-bye, it's all I can do not to drag her back to my bed like a lovesick caveman. Wanting her that bad makes me feel like a fool. "Well?" I say. "Did you get your joyous reunion?"

That gets the faucets going, a whole river of tears, but it turns out I'm not the reason she's crying. In between sobs, Holly asks me to drive her to the police station. "I have to turn myself in," she says. "I think I hit somebody." It takes her a minute to calm down enough to tell me what happened, then the words whoosh out of her like air from a slit tire. She says she finally tracked her father to a garage in Camden, only the other mechanic told her Wylie hadn't been showing up for work. That could have been the truth, or it could have been a story, and she was still trying to decide if she should stay or go as she put the truck in gear. She didn't see the mechanic stepping from between the pumps until it was too late. She swerved. There was a thump. "Maybe it wasn't him," she says. "Maybe it was just the curb." What she doesn't mention, of course, is that she was too plastered to know what happened. She'd probably been there since dawn, sitting in her pickup sipping Lord Calvert as she waited for the garage to open, working up the courage to look her old man in the eye for the first time in fifteen years.

"You think he got your license plate?"

She shrugs, wipes her eyes.

"Was anybody else around?"

She shrugs again, and that's when I realize she doesn't really want to turn herself in. But she wants it to be *my* decision not to go to the police—my problem—and pathetic as it sounds, that's all right by me. At least I'm still the one she turns to when she's in trouble.

"Relax. He probably didn't even see you," I say, "on account of your being invisible."

I've been feeling invisible myself ever since I proposed to Holly. After a week of seeing the engagement ring atop the dresser, untouched, I concluded that she didn't want to get married but wouldn't come out and say so because she wasn't ready to lose me altogether. When I tried to reassure her—when I told her that, married or not, I wasn't going anywhere—she asked why, then, had I bothered proposing?

I'd been saving for the ring all summer. I was working for Cal, fixing up the farmhouse Holly would inherit, the one she hasn't set foot in since the day we put her grandfather in the ground. Last fall, when he realized he was sick, he hired me to get the place in shape for her. She'd just started her sophomore year at Carolina and was living on campus, but she moved back to the farm in the spring, after Cal was diagnosed. Like his father, his uncle, and his grandfather, he had Alzheimer's, but unlike them, he wasn't willing to sit around waiting for his brain to go soft. Two days after we finished painting the house—the last of our projects—he took the pills. Holly had seen it coming and thought she'd talked him out of it, but then, just like that, Cal was gone.

This was in late September, and after the funeral, I proposed. She was only twenty, and I didn't want to rush things, but I wanted her to know I was there for her. We were out on the bluff, watching the sun go down. She slipped the ring on her finger and inspected it in the twilight.

"Does it fit?"

"Did you know," she said, "that half of all marriages end in divorce?"

"But that means the other half don't."

She put the ring back in the box and stared off across the soybean field Cal had turned into a driving range after he retired, the same field where her mother mastered a McCormick Farmall tractor at the age of fourteen. "I've been thinking," she said, "that I'd like to find my father."

"I'm asking you to marry me," I said.

"I know."

Holly's passed out on my bed and I want to be curled up next to her, but first I have to get the truck off the street in case the police are looking for it. Outside, it's crazy hot for November, even November in South Carolina, sunlight blazing down through the bare branches. The pickup is slouched against the curb, one tire almost flat, the windshield spattered with insects. I pull it around back and let the rest of the air out of the tire, just in case she gets any ideas about hitting the road again. Then I check the bumper, bracing for the worst. But while there are dents and scrapes and a new MURRELLS INLET IS FOR LOVERS bumper sticker, there's nothing to suggest she did anyone grievous bodily harm.

In the glove box, underneath an empty whiskey bottle and a pile of gas receipts, I find her notebook. Inside are lists of names, addresses, phone numbers—the paper trail of her search. She started looking for Wylie the day after I asked her to marry me. By then she'd packed a suitcase, locked up the farmhouse, and moved into my apartment. At the time, I thought that meant something, but it turns out all it meant was she didn't want to stay on the farm. She was supposed to be in school, but she'd skipped the first few weeks to look after Cal, and by the time he died it was too late to enroll. Maybe that was part of the problem: too much time on her hands. She spent mornings on the balcony with a bottle of wine, making phone calls and scribbling notes, calling anybody and everybody who might have a clue as to Wylie's whereabouts. When her mother died, he'd been working as a claims adjuster, so she started with the insurance agency and went from there, making her way through a list of garages, car dealerships, and boardinghouses. It seems Wylie had become something of a drifter. He also took up the habit of driving drunk, a habit Holly now sees as her birthright. The first time he landed in jail was 1979, down in Myrtle Beach. After he got out, he took a job serving papers for an attorney, a fraternity brother from his time at Carolina, but soon he went back to working on cars. Spartanburg, Chester, Florence—the list went on.

Funny thing is, for all his moving around, he's never strayed very far from home. Holly takes this as a sign. "What's keeping him here if not me?" she said one night. "I mean, why not move to some state where you're not the DUI poster boy?"

"If you're the reason," I said, "then why doesn't he come around?"

Camden's only forty miles away, but the traffic is heavy on I-20, and it's noon by the time I pull off Highway 521 and flip through Holly's notebook to double-check the address. The garage sits between two empty lots about a mile down the

road from the military academy. As I pull up to the full-
serve island, I'm relieved to see no police tape, no body out-
lined in chalk—just a sleepy Union 76 station with a handful
of cars out front waiting to be fixed. Still, it's no guarantee
some mechanic isn't laid up in the county hospital with a
busted leg.

An old guy with a cheek full of tobacco is working on a
red convertible. When he sees my car, he wipes off his hands
and heads over. "Fill 'er up?" he says.

"Please."

He puts the nozzle in and asks me to pop the hood. If
he's the mechanic Holly talked to, it's clear he hasn't been
hit by a truck, but I want to be sure. It seems too dicey to
come out and mention her, so while he's poking around the
engine, I get out of the car and tell him I'm looking for
Wylie Greer. He wipes the dipstick clean, gives me the up
and down.

"You a bill collector?"

"No," I say. "Just an old friend."

He spits onto the asphalt. "He used to work here," he
says, turning back to the car, "but now he don't. Spread the
word."

So he's the guy. I imagine the relief on Holly's face
when I tell her she's in the clear. And then, curiosity getting
the best of me, I decide to take a chance.

"That girl this morning," I say. "She's his daughter."

This gets his attention. "No kidding?" he says. "Girlie
nearly run me over."

"Really?" I apologize for any trouble Holly caused, hand
him twenty bucks, and tell him to keep the change. Then, as
I'm explaining that Holly hasn't seen her father in years,
another mechanic comes walking out of the service bay.

Even before I look, I know it's Wylie. I can picture him hanging back in the shadows, listening, waiting to make sure I'm not whoever it is he's hiding from these days—parole officer, tax man, his own daughter. "Thanks, Gene," he says, taking a rag to my windshield. "I'll finish this one up."

From the start, Holly said if I loved her, I'd help her find her father, but I couldn't bring myself to do it. I just went off to work each day, telling myself I was giving her space, hoping she'd hurry up and find him or else give up—mostly hoping she'd give up. I resented the time she spent making calls, writing letters, poring over that notebook. Some nights, when I came home beat from the old house I'd been working on, she hardly seemed to notice I was there. I told her she was wasting her time, that Wylie would have found *her* if that's what he wanted, but after a couple drinks, she'd tell me I couldn't possibly understand, seeing as how I still had a father in my life. Then she'd start making excuses for Wylie, saying how brokenhearted he must have been over losing her mother. I kept quiet, but I pictured a guy who never wanted a kid in the first place, a guy who'd turned tail and run first chance he got.

Which is why, standing there at the gas pump, I'm so surprised that Wylie chooses to show his face—and even more surprised when he invites me to lunch at the diner down the street. He offers to drive, tells me to leave my keys in case Gene needs to move the car. At the restaurant, we settle into a booth and order the special, barbecue hash and coleslaw.

"Well," Wylie says, "you're no old friend of mine, so you must be the boyfriend." He reaches across the table to shake my hand. He has Holly's freckles and red hair. He doesn't look like a guy who lives at the bottom of a bottle. His eyes are clear. His grip is a crescent wrench. "She send you up here to look for me?"

I still haven't decided whether finding him is a good thing or not, but I want to see him squirm. "She's been after you like a bloodhound."

"Why?"

I shrug. "Her grandfather—Cal—died."

"And what does that have to do with me?"

"You'd have to ask her," I say.

If I come off as rude, Wylie doesn't seem to hold it against me. In fact, when the food arrives, he asks me to tell him all about Holly, which is how we pass the next half hour, me trying to fill him in on the last fifteen years of her life. The fact that she's at Carolina, that she drives a pickup, that she wants to be a veterinarian—all of this pleases him. He's so engrossed, he barely touches his lunch, and sitting there across from him, seeing how he hangs on every detail, it's hard not to like the guy. I imagine most people who meet him must feel the same way—the housewives whose cars he fixes, the bartenders who pour him free shots, people who haven't yet known him long enough or well enough to be disappointed. When I tell him how torn up she is over Cal, he gazes out across the parking lot and lights a smoke. There was a time, he says, years ago, when he wanted Holly to come live with him in Myrtle Beach, but by then, Cal wouldn't let him near her, wouldn't even let him talk to her on the phone. "For a while, I hated that old bastard."

"Come see her," I say, wanting to know if he's sincere. "You're all the family she has left."

He glances down at the ashtray, rolls the tip of his cigarette around until it's a point. Outside, a line of cadets jog past, kicking up dust along the edge of the road. "You know, not a day passes that I don't think about her," he says. "I want to be part of her life. I really do. Just not quite yet." It's a matter of pride, he tells me. He doesn't want her to see him while he's broke and underemployed, living in a motel. He says that as soon as he gets his act together—"and it will be soon"—he's going to give her a call. He sits up straight as he says this, looking me dead in the eye like a politician, and for all I know, he actually believes what he's saying. But then he tips his hand.

"At any rate," he says, stubbing out his cigarette, "what say we keep this under our hats for now?"

He means the fact that he's still in Camden. That's when I know I was right about him all along. If Holly had come with me, he'd still be hiding in the garage. I sneak a glance at the clock over the lunch counter. If I leave soon, I could pick her up and be back in Camden before he gets off work. I'm thinking once she meets him and realizes he'll never give her what she wants, she'll be able to get on with her life—*our* life. "Sure," I say. "Just between us."

"I appreciate that."

I don't let him pay for my lunch, but when we get back to the garage, Gene is working on my car. "Oil change and a tune-up," Wylie says. "On the house." Gene isn't quite finished, so Wylie takes me out back to show off a couple of race cars he's been working on, a midget and a late model that belong to a local banker. By and by, he asks about my family. I tell him my father's in the video poker business and leave it at that. Then he wants to know how I met Holly, what line of work I'm in, whether I went to college. I'm relieved when Gene honks the horn to let us know he's done. As we turn to go back inside, Wylie clears his throat, then claps a hand on my shoulder. "So am I to understand," he says, "that you're serious about my daughter?"

The question catches me off guard. "I want to marry her."

"And vice versa?"

"Vice versa," I say, but there must be a hitch in my voice, a flicker of hesitation that lets Wylie know there's more to the story. And in that moment, as his hand drops from my shoulder, I get the feeling he sizes me up, decides then and there that though I may be important in his daughter's life, I'm not necessarily permanent. Not like blood relations. Not like him.

That look of his gnaws at me all the way home. When I walk in the door, Holly's still asleep. I pause at the foot of the bed, studying the freckles on her shoulders, the long eyelashes she inherited from her father. Maybe I'm just being paranoid, but I can't help wondering—what if Holly *is* her father's daughter? What if *I'm* the one who's never going to get what he wants? Suddenly she opens her eyes, smiles a wise-guy smile.

"May I help you?" she says.

I climb in bed and comb her hair with my fingers. I tell her I went to Camden. "Good news is, you didn't hit the guy." She looks at me like I've just lifted a car off her chest, then puts her head on my shoulder. For a few seconds, things feel like they used to back when Cal was still alive, a time when our future together seemed as inevitable as the sunrise. Then the spell's broken. She can't help herself.

"Did you ask about Wylie?"

I nod. "Same story. I guess he's gone." As soon as the words are out of my mouth, I feel like I've stepped through a rotted floorboard, but Holly doesn't doubt me. She's still focused on Gene.

"Maybe he's just covering," she says.

"Maybe," I say, and then, as long as I'm at it, I tell a second lie I hope will keep her from going back. "But the bad news is, you clipped a gas pump, and he filed a report. The cops are looking for your truck."

Holly paces around the apartment for a while, trying to puzzle out a way to get back to Camden without getting arrested, then gives up and takes a bath, which is what she always does when she's hung over. While she's in the tub, I sit at the kitchen table, smoking bent cigarettes from the crumpled pack in her purse. Her father is out there. I saw him, I ate a meal with him, I shook his hand, and now I've taken it upon myself to see that she doesn't get to do the same. *Who the hell do you think you are?* I can hear the fury in her voice. Because sooner or later, she'll learn the truth. And what will my excuse be? That I was only doing what I thought was best? That I was honoring Wylie's wishes? I'm tempted to walk into the bathroom and just come clean, but not tempted enough. So I sit there, knowing that in a few minutes, she'll emerge from the steam scrubbed and sweet-smelling, and we'll carry on in our limbo until she either runs off again, or figures out I lied to her, or both. It occurs to me I have a finite amount of time before the shit hits the fan, time I can't afford to waste. What we need, I decide, is a change of scenery.

As soon as Holly turns on the hair dryer, I call the lady in

Shandon whose kitchen I've been redoing to tell her I won't be at work for a few days, then I quickly pack a duffel bag and sneak it into the trunk of my car. I'm back at the table smoking another cigarette when Holly sulks into the kitchen in jeans and a black T-shirt. She pours a glass of water and pops some aspirin.

"I'm starved," she says. "Let's order a pizza."

"Let's go out for one."

We're halfway to the farm before Holly realizes where we're headed. She doesn't want to go. She tells me she's not ready. "Turn around," she says, "or let me out right here." I have to hold her wrist at the next stoplight to keep her in the car. I try reasoning with her, reminding her that the mail is piling up, food's rotting in the fridge, the lawn is going to seed.

"If you're so concerned," she says, "you deal with it."

I keep driving. I know she's not a child, but I do believe that what Holly needs, now and then, is someone to take charge, someone to guide her down the path she's too scared to go down herself. "Not going there isn't going to make Cal not be dead," I say.

She closes her eyes, takes a deep breath. "First of all," she says, "this has nothing to do with Cal. This is about me and you. You think we're going to get out there, just the two of us, and it's going to be like old times, and suddenly I'll decide I'm ready to get married."

I keep my eyes on the road, trying not to let on that she's nailed me. "And second of all?"

"Second of all, fuck you. I don't want to go." Saying the words seems to cement her anger, and when we get to the farm, she lets herself into the house and locks me out. I stand there knocking for a few minutes. Through the door, she informs me that I'm trespassing and that if I don't leave, she'll call the police. I knock some more. When she finally opens up, she's holding Cal's Daisy rifle, the one he kept around to scare off the neighbor's hogs when they got loose in his garden.

"Get off my property," she says.

"Whoa. That's a pretty mean-looking BB gun."

She raises her eyebrows, clicks off the safety, and shoots me in the thigh. It stings—more than I would've expected—and when I reach for the gun, she shoots me in the hand. She's back inside with the door locked before I can stop her. Next thing I know, she's opening an upstairs window, taking aim at me again. I can tell she's enjoying this.

"Suit yourself," I say. "Good luck." As I'm walking away, she shoots my windshield, leaving a neat, milky divot in the glass. I lean against the car, trying to rub the sting out of my hand as I scope out the house. The downstairs windows are low enough to break into, plus I'm pretty sure Cal kept a key under the doormat. It would be easy to get inside, but after lying to Holly and dragging her out here, I figure she deserves to win this round. If she wants to shoot me and lock me out, fine, whatever, I'll come back later. My only concern is that she'll take off while I'm gone. There's not much I can do if she decides to call a taxi or walk back to town, but I don't want her getting behind the wheel, so, before I leave, I slip into the barn and disconnect the battery on Cal's old Plymouth.

It's dark by the time I get back with the pizza. Through the window, I see Holly sitting in the dining room, going through a box of old photographs and arranging them in stacks across the table. She lets me in when she sees I have food. Her eyes are red from crying. Taking my hand, she traces the welt on my palm with the tip of her finger. "I'm sorry I shot you," she says. "Do you want to shoot me?"

"Maybe later." I give her a kiss and open the cupboard for a couple of plates, but she asks me not to.

"I want to leave things the way they are," she says. "Let's just eat outside."

I follow her out front, where she sets the pizza and her pint bottle on the wrought-iron table beneath one of the live oaks beside the driveway. This is where we used to sit with Cal for cocktails every Friday afternoon, the very spot where Holly and I first met. I pull a chair up next to her and reach for the Lord Calvert. She does, too, probably afraid I'll pour it out, but instead I take a long swallow and pass it back to her. We haven't been drunk together since the day of the funeral.

"What say we get loaded?"

She gives a halfhearted laugh. "Already there."

That's the last thing she says until the pizza's gone. By then it's almost nine o'clock. She's a wreck, just sitting there staring at the house, dabbing her eyes with a tissue, and it makes me queasy to think what she'd do if she knew her father was just forty miles away, downing his own nightly ration. When I offer to take her back to my apartment, she shakes her head. She has decided, after all, that this is where she belongs, here on the farm where her mother and Cal lived, the only place where she still feels connected to them. At least, that's how I imagine she feels. She stands up and announces she's going back inside to finish sorting the photographs. I offer to help, but she says she'd rather do it alone. By midnight, she still hasn't come to bed. I find her at the dining room table, asleep, with a stack of photos next to her. The one on top is a snapshot of Holly, her mother, and Cal posed on the front steps, three generations in their Sunday best. It's a photo I've seen before, taken on Easter Day, 1976, a few months before Maddy died. Wylie was there, too—he's the one behind the camera. If you look closely, you can see the faint shadow he casts.

The next morning, I wake to the sound of Holly playing back messages that have accumulated on Cal's answering machine. I sit up, ready for disaster. What if one of the messages is from Wylie? What if he called to say meeting me made him want to see her? I dress quickly and head downstairs, listening, but the calls are from friends of hers, people wanting to offer condolences. Even so, bringing her to the farm now seems like a mistake, because of course if Wylie has a change of heart, it's the first place he'll look.

"Why don't we go out for brunch?" I say. "Maybe see a movie."

Holly's sitting on Cal's bed, jotting notes. She tells me she's already eaten and doesn't have time for a movie. "I've got a lot of stuff to take care of here," she says, "but you could give me a ride into town to get my clothes."

It takes a moment for what she's saying to sink in. "You're moving out?"

She pats my hand, which still smarts from the BB. "I never moved in," she says. "I was just staying at your place. And now you can stay here for a while, if you want."

This is what I've been hoping for all along—the two of us together on the farm—but Holly refuses to make a big deal of it. She just turns back to the answering machine. "I want to get my truck, too."

"I meant to tell you. It's got a flat."

"So we'll get it fixed."

"Maybe we should wait," I say. "The police are looking for it, remember?"

That's when Holly informs me she's going back to Camden, with or without my help. It's no use trying to talk her out of it. I take a seat beside her, sinking into the old mattress. "What do you want me to do?"

"Take me there tomorrow," she says, which must have been her plan all along, the threat of her driving just a threat to get a ride. As she's erasing the messages, she tells me she had a dream last night. She was back at the garage in her pickup, just like Saturday morning, only this time, the man she almost hit was her father. "I think he's still there," she says. "I can feel it."

"That's not what old Gene said."

"But here's what I don't get," she says. "If he called the cops, and if he knew you knew where to find me, why didn't he call them again so they could question you?"

"Maybe he'd cooled off by then."

"Or maybe he just made up that stuff about the police. To scare you off."

"It's possible."

"Well," she says, "only one way to find out."

It takes Holly less than fifteen minutes to pack up the two suitcases of clothes she's been keeping at my apartment, and then we head back to the farm in my car. She's okay with leaving the truck now that I've agreed to drive her to

Camden. As we're passing the VA hospital, she asks me to stop at the cemetery up ahead. She hasn't been there since the funeral. We don't stay long—just long enough for her to smoke a cigarette and get rid of the dead flowers on Cal's grave—and she doesn't pray or cry, just stands there scowling at the headstone.

As soon as we're at the house, she puts on a pot of coffee and gets to work. She starts by opening all the windows, then she strips Cal's bed and gathers up his towels. When I ask if there's anything I shouldn't touch, she just shoves another blanket into the washer. "He didn't want this place to be a museum," she says. "He wanted us to *live* here." I'm happy to hear her say "us," but that's the only bone she throws me. The rest of the day she's moody, preoccupied with the task at hand. Once we've emptied the closets, we pack up Cal's clothes and store them in the attic alongside boxes of her mother's belongings. Next we start going through dressers and cabinets, sorting his personal effects. Most of his stuff gets packed away, but some of it Holly keeps out—his tackle box, his Carhartt coat with the wool lining, a silver flask we find in the nightstand. It's a slow process, trying to decide how much of her grandfather she still wants around, and Holly doesn't take it well. By lunchtime, she's on her third glass of wine. All the while, I'm resigned to the fact that we're going back to Camden, and every time I pass through Cal's room and see her notebook next to the phone, I could kick myself. Because now that we're here together, just the two of us, I don't see how Wylie was even worth lying about.

In the morning, Holly's sitting up in bed, watching me. My first thought is, I've been talking in my sleep, spilling the beans about Wylie, but when I ask her what's wrong, she tells me she couldn't sleep. "Let's go," she says. "I want to be there when they open." Again, I try to talk her into waiting— "just to let things cool off," I say—and when that doesn't work, I tell her it's risky to show up first thing in the morning. "We don't want him to see us staking out the place," I say. "He might turn around and go home." I finally convince her to wait until after lunch. Even so, she's antsy. As soon as she finishes breakfast, she mixes a bloody mary and picks up where she left off the day before, sorting through Cal's desk. Passing the doorway, I notice she's wearing the engagement ring. She glances up from a stack of old bank statements, gives me a look that says, *Now don't get all excited.*

"I'm just trying it on for size," she says. "The whole idea."

As much as I like the look of that ring on her finger, I'm too nervous to sit still, so when she asks if I want to help clean out the desk, I tell her no thanks, I'll be mowing the grass. I start with the front yard, which has come to look more like a wild meadow than the neat lawn Cal once kept. The grass is still wet with dew, and I'm so busy thinking about Wylie that I keep stalling the mower. My only hope is that he won't be at work, or that he'll pretend we never met, seeing as how that was his idea in the first place. More likely, though, he'll assume I told Holly where he was, in which case he'll have little incentive to cover for me, the temporary boyfriend of his permanent daughter.

Around lunchtime, on my way back to the shed for the gas can, I notice the barn door is open. My mouth goes dry. Inside, Holly is under the hood of Cal's Plymouth. She sees me coming and bangs the hood shut. Then she gets in and locks the doors. I realize she's on to me somehow, though it won't be until later, when she visits me in the Kershaw County Jail, that I'll learn the whole story, how she got impatient after her third bloody mary and dialed up the garage. A man answered the phone, and even though Holly hung up without a word, not wanting to spook him, she was certain the voice on the other end was her father's. She wondered how he'd managed to duck me when I was in Camden. She thought about all the times I'd tried to talk her out of looking for him. She put two and two together. It was only a hunch, but with a few drinks in her, that was enough.

Now she's trying to start the car, which has been in the barn gathering dust since springtime, when Cal stopped driving. His silver flask is on the seat next to her. I figure my best bet is to play dumb, so I stand there tapping on the window, asking her what's going on, asking her to open up. She tries the ignition again. When the engine finally turns over, blue smoke billows from the tailpipe and a clutch of swallows burst from the rafters. Holly throws the car into reverse, backs out of the barn, and stops long enough to pull the diamond ring off her finger. For a moment she just sits there, holding it in her fist, and then she rolls down the window and drops it in the dirt.

By the time I get on I-20, Holly's nowhere to be seen. I figure she's only a half mile ahead of me, tops, but I hang back, fighting the urge to catch up. I don't want her to spot my car; I don't want her trying to outrun me. As it is, I'm sure she's hauling ass, drunk enough to pretend she's invisible, and every time I come around a bend in the road, I expect to see her being handcuffed at the back of a cruiser. It's no surprise, then, just a mile or so before Camden, when I crest a hill in time to spot a state trooper pulling onto the highway, lights twirling. I speed up, trying to see who he's after, but it's not until the exit is in sight that I make out the Plymouth. Holly isn't slowing down a bit. She flies up the ramp, brakes hard, and hangs a sharp left at the light. The trooper gets stuck behind a big RV at the exit, and then he has to wait while an eighteen-wheeler makes a wide, slow turn onto the overpass. By now Holly has disappeared. The trooper turns off his siren and slows down, probably calling for backup. I'm only a few blocks behind him, heading past the academy, when he makes a wrong turn down a side street.

I let out my breath for what seems like the first time in hours. It's too late for wishing Holly had pulled over, so now I'm just hoping she makes it to the garage without wrapping the car around a telephone pole. That, and I'm hoping she has the sense to park behind the building, out of sight. But two minutes later, when I pull into the lot, the Plymouth is sitting right out front, blocking the service bay. The door is wide open, and the flask is lying on the front seat for all the world to see. Holly's already inside. She shoots me a fierce look through the plate-glass window, then turns back to Gene, who's cornered behind the register. Her voice carries through the garage. "Don't give me that," she's saying. "He was here half an hour ago. He answered the phone."

Scanning the parking lot, I expect to see Wylie's Firebird, expect to see Wylie himself, but the only other person around is a teenager gassing up his VW. It's all I can do to keep calm. I don't even want to consider the possibility that Wylie's gone, because if Holly really knows I lied, it'll be my fault he got away. I cut through the garage, casting a quick glance around. Before now, it hasn't occurred to me that Wylie might have skipped town, but suddenly it makes perfect sense. Of course he figured I'd tell Holly I found him. Of course he didn't think I'd lie to the woman I love.

Now Holly regards me with mock surprise. "How about that?" she says. "Another liar." Gene looks like he's swallowed a mouthful of Beech-Nut. He turns to me for help, as though Holly is mine to control, but she's already stepping through the doorway behind the register. I can hear other doors opening as she searches the office, the bathroom, the break room. I catch up with her as she pushes through the back door out into the dusty lot behind the garage.

"Will you please stop following me?" she says. We're standing between the two race cars Wylie's been working on. I tell Holly that if she'll calm down for five seconds, I'll explain. She surprises me by crossing her arms and waiting. "One one thousand," she says, eyes boring into me. "Two one thousand." I'm still trying to decide where to start when I hear tires screeching. I crack the door. Two state patrol cars have converged on the garage, blocking the Plymouth. When the troopers get out, they have their revolvers drawn, and they don't look happy: somebody has embarrassed them, and somebody's going to pay.

One glance over my shoulder and Holly's ready to run, but I've got her by the arm and I'm not letting go. I press my car keys into her hand. "Give me yours," I say. She starts to argue, but I tell her to hurry, it'll be worse for her. She's shaking so hard she can barely get the keys out of her pocket. The last thing I do before I walk through that door is close her fingers around the diamond ring.

The troopers are barricaded behind their cars, calling for the driver of the Plymouth to come out of the building with his hands up, so that's what I do. Gene's still at the register, and I'm afraid he'll blow Holly's cover, but he gives me a glance as I pass, sums up the situation with a raised eyebrow, and spits into a Coke bottle. For all the headache Holly's caused him, he is not a man without pity—at least when it comes to his buddy's daughter.

As soon as I'm out front, the troopers start yelling at me to get down. I drop to my knees, then lie facedown on the asphalt beside the gas pumps. They're on me in a flash, pinning me and cuffing my hands behind my back. All the while they're calling me cowboy, telling me what a fuckup I am, how badly I fucked up, how fucked I am. I keep my mouth shut and stare straight ahead, hoping for a glimpse of Holly at the back door, but what catches my eye instead, underneath a van in the service bay, is a dark figure—the figure, perhaps, of a mechanic lying on a creeper. Then again, maybe it's just a shadow. I blink twice, squinting through the shimmers of heat rising from the blacktop, but before I know for sure what I'm looking at, the trooper takes his boot off my back and they're hauling me up, guiding me toward the cruiser. I want to call out to Holly, tell her to look under the van, but I don't want the police to see her. It's hard to swallow the fact that I'll never know if that's Wylie under there. I'd like to think it is. I'd like to think he and Holly are taking a good long look as the troopers bend me into the back of the car, and what they're seeing, both of them, is a guy who's not afraid to put in his time.

CHAPTER FOUR

1970

Wylie

Wylie knew Maddy didn't intend to spend the rest of her life banging fenders with a bunch of dirt dobbers and shade-tree mechanics in some little bullring. "You and me," she told him, "we got a plan." Really, it was more pipe dream than plan, but Wylie didn't care, so long as he was in it. Basically it involved the two of them leaving Columbia and running off to North Carolina. That's where they'd build their first real car, a late-model sportsman. No more hobby division. Wylie would be the mechanic, crew chief, whatever: he'd take care of the car. Maddy would do what she did best, which was drive. Her goal was to make the Grand National circuit, become the first lady driver at Darlington. Together, they'd be NASCAR's only husband and wife team.

"If we've got a plan," Wylie said, "what are we waiting for?"

It was Thursday afternoon, Maddy's day off, and they were in the four-poster bed paid for by her fiancé, Dale—a big bed for the big house Dale planned to buy once they were married. Maddy still hadn't told Dale they were through, and Wylie was starting to think she never would. He nudged her hip with his.

"Well?"

"You tell me," Maddy said.

This was what came after the sex, the two of them saying the same things they'd been saying to each other for months. It was a conversation that went around and around, like a slow, frustrating race, only there was no finish line in sight. He wanted her to leave Dale, she wanted him to leave Sheila, but no matter how many threats or pleas or ultimatums were spoken, neither had the nerve to make the first move.

Now they had an hour before they had to be at the track, back in the real world, and they might have wasted the rest of the afternoon arguing if someone hadn't rung the doorbell. For a second Maddy stared at Wylie as if she didn't quite believe what she'd heard, then she flew out of bed and started throwing on her clothes. Wylie's first impulse was to hide in the closet, which he wasn't too proud to do, but he was too proud to get caught there, so he concentrated on not losing his cool. It made his heart pound to think about the world of shit he was in for if Sheila found out how he spent his Thursday afternoons. There would be tears and shouting, maybe flying bottles. She'd want to know who else knew, why he hadn't told her the truth, when he'd quit loving her, what she'd done to make him hate her enough to make such a fool of her. She'd want to know about the sex, too—how many times they'd done it, what was so great about it, so great about Maddy. Then *she'd* probably want to do it, which he'd probably feel obliged to do, and the whole time she'd be crying and asking him why, and he wouldn't have a single thing to say for himself.

"Sheila's at work," he said, pulling on his jeans. "Dale's at work. It's probably somebody selling something."

Maddy was feeling under the bed for her bra. "Of *course* it's not Dale. Dale has a key."

Wylie didn't let himself think too hard about the fact that *he* didn't have a key. He peered between the curtains and found himself staring down at the orange crew cut of Bobby Taggert, one of the other mechanics from the Ford dealership they all worked at. That morning, after replacing the transmission in a Galaxie, Wylie'd told Tag he was off to deliver a fuel pump to a speed shop out in Lexington. Over in parts, Maddy had had the pump waiting. Now it was on the seat of Wylie's truck just around the corner, still in its box, and for all Wylie knew, Tag had seen it and figured out the score.

Tag rang the doorbell again. His race car, a dented 1959 Fairlane, was hitched to the back of his Jeep at the curb. It was the same model as Maddy's, only three years older and worse for wear. "Maddy? Wylie? Anybody home?"

Maddy covered her mouth when she recognized the voice. "Oh my God," she said. "Why's he calling you?"

All Wylie could do was shrug. Between work and the track, Tag saw them together more than anybody else. The three of them used to spend weekends in Maddy's driveway, tinkering with the Fairlanes while Sheila and Dale drank beer and tossed horseshoes in the yard. But Maddy hadn't been on speaking terms with Tag since he knocked her out of last week's race. She didn't believe for a second it had been an accident. "Those boys put him up to it," she'd told Wylie as her car was towed off the track. "I guarantee you, they took up a collection, drew straws or something to see who'd be the lucky guy."

Wylie'd thought she was wrong about Tag—all week the poor guy had been apologizing for the wreck—but now, gazing down at Tag's sunburned forehead, he wasn't so sure. It was no secret the other drivers wanted Maddy gone, and with the cold shoulder she'd been giving Tag, it was only a matter of time before he started feeling the same. So maybe he was here to yank their chain a little; maybe he was even thinking there was some money to be made. Or maybe it was nothing like that at all. Maybe he just figured Maddy would be out for revenge—a pretty safe bet—and he was here to patch things up.

"You should go see what he wants," Wylie said.

Maddy looked like he'd asked her to jump out the window. "*I'm* not going down there."

"Never mind," Wylie said. "He's leaving."

But he wasn't. He was heading around back, where Maddy's Fairlane was parked in front of the garage. She and Wylie tiptoed across the hall and watched from the bathroom as Tag climbed into her car, gripped the wheel, and spat tobacco juice into the gravel. *Get your freckly ass out of my car,* Wylie thought. True, Dale was the Fairlane's actual owner, but Wylie was the one who kept it running. Wylie was the one who'd used up a week's vacation turning it into a race car, five days he was supposed to spend at Garden City with Sheila, five days he was still catching hell for.

"That son of a bitch," Maddy said, squinting between the blinds.

"He's not doing anything. He's just sitting there."

"What if he starts poking around under the hood?" She was worried about the roller-tappet cam, the milled cylinder heads, all of the stuff she hadn't wanted done to the car but that Wylie had insisted on doing, telling her they had to bend a rule here and there because all the other drivers did, too.

"He won't find anything," Wylie said. "He'd have to take the whole engine apart."

Maddy was threatening to call the police by the time Tag finally hoisted himself from the car. For a moment he stared at the house, as if waiting for Maddy to show herself, then he shrugged, walked into the garage, and came out carrying Wylie's socket kit. Wylie put his arm around Maddy. "See? He's just borrowing tools."

"You mean stealing." Maddy ducked away and headed back to the bedroom. From behind the curtain, they watched Tag stash the socket kit in the Jeep and pull away. Before he made the turn onto Rosewood, he stuck his arm out the window. A turn signal? A wave? A taunt? Maddy sat on the bed with her hands between her knees. It was ninety degrees out, but she was shivering. "I can't believe this," she said. "I can't believe you're so calm. He's *spying* on us."

"Who's calm?" Wylie said, but she was right—he felt almost peaceful. Watching Tag drive off, he'd begun to think maybe this wasn't such a bad turn of events. If Tag did know about them, and if that led to Dale finding out, then Maddy would have to make a decision. Really, it would be for her own good. She wasn't meant to be with Dale, but she couldn't bring herself to leave him. "How can I do that to him?" she'd say. "We're supposed to get married and have kids and spend summers at Hilton Head." Dale owned Holman's, the downtown men's shop he'd taken over from his father. He was a nice guy who could provide a nice life for Maddy. But it seemed that what Wylie and Maddy had was true love, and it seemed, too, a lot of the time, that Maddy wouldn't be able to live without it. Still, there were other times when it seemed like Maddy had her eyes on the prize, the fat life with Dale, and Wylie was just a way to pass the time.

"Maybe this is a sign," he said. "Maybe we should tell Sheila and Dale before Tag does."

Maddy glared at him. "A sign?" she said. "There aren't any *signs*, Wylie." She picked up his shirt and shoes and shoved them against his stomach.

"But won't it be worse if they hear it from someone else?"

"Out," she said, steering him into the hall and closing the door. Wylie stood in the hallway with his forehead against the door, listening to Maddy bang drawers shut. In trying to force her hand, he had crossed a line. Normally, that was Dale's department—Dale who was so sure he knew what was best for Maddy, that she should quit racing, leave parts, take some classes, or come work at Holman's. When it was quiet again, Wylie went in. She was lying on her side, facing the wall. Her uniform—gray coveralls with red stripes stitched down the sides—was draped over the footboard. Wylie sat next to her and gathered up the damp hair at the back of her neck, blowing a little breeze there.

"My life is one big mistake," she said.

"No, it's not," he said. "It's a series of small mistakes."

She smiled a little, and he apologized and said of course they shouldn't tell Dale and Sheila, not unless it was what they both wanted, and before long he had her across the hall and in the shower. "What for?" she said. "I'm just going to get filthy at the track," but she let him soap up her back and shampoo her hair. He told her to relax, focus on the race. When he'd finished rinsing her off, he patted her down with a towel. They were back at the window looking out at the Fairlane. Wylie couldn't afford an Ethan Allen bed, so this had been his birthday present to her—a gleaming silver paint job worthy of a Grand National car, her number eleven in black on each door, and, along the fenders, trails of flame the color of her hair. The first time she saw it, she looked like she wanted to cry. "It's so pretty," she'd said. "And it'll just get banged to shit."

The track was in West Columbia, out past Piggie Park Bar-B-Q on 321 South. As they approached the gate, Wylie told Maddy he wanted to touch up the Ford on Saturday. That, and he'd like a key to her apartment. She leaned over, kissed him, and slipped him a key. "Keep it somewhere safe," she said, as if she'd been planning to give him one all along. At the gate, she flashed her NASCAR license, and the sleepy attendant waved them across the track and into the infield. The grandstand was already starting to fill up. This was 1970, before they paved the track and people stopped coming. Wylie drove past the shiny late-models on pit row and headed for the cusp of infield grass that served as a makeshift pit area for the hobby cars. Guys in T-shirts and grease-smeared jeans were tuning battered Fords and Chevys. All of the cars were old, and all of them were American; those were the rules in the hobby division. A couple of guys nodded hello to Wylie, but nobody came over, which was how it had been ever since he hooked up with Maddy. Columbia Speedway was one of the few tracks around that allowed women on pit row, but there were no women owners, no women mechanics, and certainly no other women drivers, not unless you counted powder-puff derbies, and Maddy didn't.

As Wylie was getting her car unhooked from the pickup, he spotted Tag towing his own Ford across the track. Wylie waved.

"What are you doing?" Maddy said.

"Acting normal. Till he gives me a reason not to."

"Like wrecking me? Or snooping around my house?"

She started for the pit office to pay her entry fee, cutting between parked cars so she wouldn't have to cross paths with Tag. He pulled up behind Wylie's pickup, revving his engine for a joke, as if his old Jeep were some hot rod. "Borrow your eyes for a minute?"

"Sure." Wylie followed the Jeep down the row until Tag found a place to park, then guided him as he backed in. Tag was holding Wylie's socket kit when he got out.

"Hope you don't mind," he said. "I stopped by Maddy's, but nobody was home."

Wylie expected a knowing look, a wise-ass smile, but Tag was already digging around behind his seat, pulling out a box of spark plugs, explaining that he'd never have taken the tools without asking, but he was in a pinch because he'd cut out of work early to tune up his car, but like a damn moron he'd forgotten to bring his toolbox home. "Mind if I quick throw these in?"

"Take your time."

Tag kept up a steady chatter as he worked. He said he was glad to see Maddy's car back in one piece, and then he apologized for the umpteenth time about the wreck. Wylie told him it was no big deal, just some dents and a flat tire, but Tag wouldn't let it drop. "Track didn't have much bite, did it?" he said. "Not that that's any excuse." He was just putting in the last spark plug when he glanced up and saw Maddy. She was carrying a cardboard tray with two Cokes and a bag of chips, giving them a wide berth on her way back to the pickup.

"Hey there, Maddy," he hollered. "I was just telling Wylie how bad I feel about last week."

Maddy slowed down, and for a second Wylie thought she might forgive and forget. "Gosh, Tag," she said. "That's so white of you."

"Jesus." Tag turned to Wylie. "See how she talks to me?"

Maddy was already walking off. Wylie knew she didn't want him apologizing for her, but he couldn't help himself. "Forget it," he said. "You know how she gets before a race."

Tag scratched at his ear. "If you say so."

On the way back to the pickup, Wylie scanned the top row of the grandstand, where Sheila and Dale always sat. It was almost time for the practice laps to start, and usually they were at the track by now, settling in with foamy cups of beer. Sometimes, if there was a good song on the PA, Sheila would be up on the bleachers, dancing with little kids. Dale was usually making bets on the feature with whoever was sitting nearby, passing out sticks of licorice-flavored chewing gum.

"You seen Dale and Sheila?"

Maddy shook her head. She was on the tailgate, sipping her Coke and staring at the Ford. She didn't look happy. Through the windshield, Wylie saw a jockstrap draped over the steering wheel. Last week it had been a French tickler, and the week before that, a ratty pair of men's briefs. Now the whole pit was watching Maddy, hoping to see her lose it. Instead, she just strolled over to the car, tucked the jockstrap into her pocket, and came back to the tailgate. You'd have had to be standing as close as Wylie was to see the tremor in her hands. Now the other drivers were grinning and elbowing each other. Wylie sat down beside Maddy, eyeing them until they looked away.

"You okay?" he said.

"Fine." She tore open the chips. She'd have preferred

peanuts, but they were considered bad luck on pit row—even on the half-assed hobby pit row.

"Someday you'll be running at Daytona," Wylie said, "and all these clowns'll still be right here."

Maddy wasn't in the mood for a pep talk. "So what did Tag say?"

Wylie told her Tag's story, said he didn't think Tag knew a thing.

"But that doesn't explain why he was calling your name," she said.

"I could have stopped by to pick you up."

"Or why he didn't just wait until he got here to borrow the tools."

"Maybe we should forget about Tag, concentrate on the race."

"I hope the little prick gets drafted," Maddy said.

They were still working on their Cokes and sizing up the competition when Wylie spotted Sheila and Dale coming across the infield with a cooler between them. He scooted away from Maddy, then wished he hadn't, because of course it only made him look like he had something to hide.

"Surprise!" Sheila called out. She was wearing what passed for a uniform at the record store where she worked—low-slung jeans, a flowery little blouse, no bra. As usual, Dale looked like he belonged at a country club. He had on a yellow golf shirt, loafers, the plaid slacks he sold at his store. By now the hobby crowd was used to his clothes, but the drivers still didn't see how any man could love a girl who drove a race car. "Poor guy," they'd say. "You think he ever gets to be on top?"

As soon as Sheila set down her end of the cooler, she gave

Wylie a long, complicated kiss, the kind that turns heads. He could feel Maddy standing there like a storm cloud, watching, and he thought about what she always said, that Sheila acted this way because she was trying to hold on. He kissed Sheila like he meant it.

"Aren't you going to lose your seats?" Maddy said.

Dale shrugged, slapped dust from the flared leg of his slacks. Normally he and Sheila didn't come down until after the races, when the four of them headed across the highway for drinks at the Checkered Flag. "We got tired of being racing widows. Thought we might watch down here."

"Don't worry," Sheila said. "We'll stay out of the way."

Wylie forced a smile. "Who's worried?"

After Maddy took her practice laps, the four of them spent the next hour kicked back in lawn chairs, watching the heats and waiting for the hobby race. Dale kept a hand on Maddy's knee like he owned it—like he didn't even have to think about owning it. Twice Wylie caught himself staring, thinking how he'd like to bend Dale's fingers back to his fancy gold watch, and twice he told himself that when all was said and done, he'd be the one sitting next to Maddy. And dependable Dale, bless his heart, he was paving the way. Dale had never been able to watch Maddy race. Every week, he left Sheila in the bleachers and paced behind the grandstand, chewing his Black Jack and chain-smoking until the race was over. Last week at the Flag, after a couple pitchers, he'd turned to Wylie, genuinely baffled. "You're her friend. How can you let her go out there?" The question had caught Wylie off guard. If he wasn't as protective of Maddy as Dale was, did that mean he loved her less?

Maddy interrupted. "Nobody 'lets' me go out there," she said. "Anyhow, *you* bought the car."

Dale reached for the pitcher and allowed that yes, he'd bought the car, and maybe he'd sell it, too. "I just wanted you to get it out of your system." She kissed him on the cheek and told him she was working on it, which was a lie. The only reason she let Dale think otherwise was because she wanted to keep her options open.

Now Wylie shifted his chair so he wouldn't have to look at the two of them. Sheila was trolling the cooler again. She'd been throwing back beers, but Wylie hadn't said a word, because she drank like that only when she had a reason, and he didn't want to know what it was. As she cracked open another one, she noticed Wylie eyeing her and made a show of pooling herself like honey into his lap. Later, of course, Maddy would accuse him of enjoying it—never mind the way she'd been cozying up to Dale.

Every chance Sheila got, she flagged down whoever happened to be walking by and invited them over for a beer. Most of the other drivers knew her. She'd been voted track queen two years running, and even Dale had trouble keeping his eyes off her. Pretty soon there was a small group at the back of the pickup. The few drivers who bothered saying hey to Maddy didn't say much more. They were too busy falling all over themselves being sweet to Sheila. Maddy looked like she was at a funeral. When Tag strolled over to join the party, she slipped away and stood alone by the track, watching the last late-model heat, no doubt feeling sorry for herself. Wylie almost went after her, but then he looked at Dale and thought, screw it—it was Maddy's turn to feel bad. Maybe if she felt bad enough long enough, she'd get off the fence. He rested his chin on Sheila's shoulder, whispered that

he loved her. He didn't mean it—not the way he used to—
but it felt good to say it. It felt like he had options, too.

When the announcer called for the hobby cars to take the
track, Dale helped Maddy adjust her chin strap and asked
her to be careful, reminding her how lucky she'd been to
walk away from last week's wreck.

"Jesus H.," she said. "Is this my first race?"

Wylie couldn't help it—he loved when she snapped at
Dale—but he knew he was the one she was really mad at.
Wouldn't look at him, wouldn't talk to him. And now he felt
sure she'd do something stupid on the track, just to get back
at him. He leaned in and wished her good luck, but she just
stared straight ahead and put the car in gear. As she joined the
other cars leaving the pit area, she tucked a stray wisp of hair
up under her helmet, and Wylie could hardly believe he'd
been in her shower just three hours ago with his hands in her
hair, her skin against his. Sometimes he wasn't sure who he
was anymore, which life he was living.

Tag was two cars behind Maddy. As he drove by, he
winked at Sheila, who was leaning against the pickup, then
grinned and winked at Wylie to show he didn't mean any
harm. Once the track stewards got the cars lined up, Dale
headed for the concession stand. Wylie and Sheila climbed
into the back of the truck and watched as the drivers slowly
circled the dirt oval. Now that they were alone, Sheila had
gone silent and sullen.

"It's good having company for a change," Wylie said.

"Pass me the binoculars?" She kept her eyes on the track
as the green flag dropped, the cars bucking forward, gouging
the air, swaying like sheet-metal winos on their soft springs.

It was the usual hobby division slop, three spinouts and two wrecks before the end of the first lap, but Sheila hardly seemed to notice. She had the binoculars trained on Maddy even when she sipped her beer. Wylie told himself she was just in a mood—she'd had too much to drink on a hot night was all. But he wished she'd say something. She was making him nervous.

Maddy was, too. She was driving like a fool, weaving pell-mell through traffic, sailing full tilt into the turns. He hoped she'd ease up long enough to think about what she was doing. They weren't even close to having enough money to build a car yet. If she blew the engine or crashed, they'd be done for the season—unless Dale ponied up for another ride, which didn't seem likely.

After eleven laps, only half the field was left. Maddy had worked her way up to third behind Tag, who was chopping her, trying like the rest of the drivers not to let her pass. When she closed in on him, Wylie knew what was coming, he just didn't know how bad it would be. Maddy got inside Tag going into the second turn and let her front end tap his rear fender. It was enough to send him fishtailing into her path. Sheila jumped up, squeezing Wylie's arm as Tag glanced off the rail and spun. By some miracle, Maddy avoided plowing into him, and by the time his car came to rest, she was already halfway down the backstretch, dogging the lead car. The infield crowd swelled toward the wreck as the flagman waved a blur of red.

"She did that on purpose," Sheila said.

"No, ma'am. The car must be pushing."

But of course Sheila was right. There was nothing wrong with Maddy's suspension; she could easily have blown past Tag. Instead, Tag's car was now crumpled against the rail, facing traffic, smoke curling from its hood. Maddy was lucky she didn't get black-flagged. As she and the other drivers pulled over to let the wrecker pass, Wylie told himself she'd only done it because she was scared and frustrated, but no matter how he looked at it, there was just no excuse. It was a relief when Tag climbed out of the car. He seemed to be in one piece. He pitched his helmet into the dirt and waved off help from the stewards, which got him a cheer from the crowd. While they were busy winching the car onto the wrecker, Wylie took a crescent wrench from his toolbox, rolled it up in an old newspaper, and set it across his lap. Even though it was Tag and Tag was a buddy, there was always hell to pay for a wreck, and he wanted to be ready.

Sheila shook her head. "Why don't you let Dale look after her?"

"I'm looking after myself."

She tossed an empty can into the corner of the truck bed and mumbled something under her breath. It sounded like, "I bet you are."

Maddy ended up winning, her fifth checkered flag of the season, tops among the hobby drivers. She was taking a victory lap when Dale came back from the concession stand, asking if she was all right, saying he'd heard about the wreck. He was carrying enough hot dogs for everyone.

"She's fine," Wylie said. "She won."

Sheila'd seen enough. She handed the binoculars to Dale. By now Maddy was steering back toward the pickup, in no hurry at all, the jockstrap dangling like a pendant from her rearview for all the other drivers to see. When she parked and pulled off her helmet, she was beaming. Winning a race always fixed whatever was wrong in her life. Usually it did the same for Wylie, but not tonight. As soon as she was out of the car, he let her see the wrench. Tag would be along any minute, and Wylie wanted to make sure she understood the position she'd put him in. If there was a fight, it would be his butt on the line, not hers. Tag wouldn't hit a girl.

"Don't give me that look," Maddy said. "I can't afford to turn the other cheek out there."

"Hold on," Dale said, setting down the hot dogs. "What happened exactly?"

Sure enough, Tag was already headed their way, a small crowd streaming out behind him like exhaust smoke. Sheila hopped down from the truck, pushed past Wylie, and intercepted Tag. She threw her arms around him as if he'd just come back from the war. She fussed over the cut on his chin, asking if it hurt, if he was okay. He managed a grin. "Only scratch on me," he said. Then his grin was gone and he was in Maddy's face, asking what her problem was. He turned so red you almost couldn't make out his freckles.

Maddy didn't back down. "Now you know how it feels," she said.

Wylie was about to step in when Dale beat him to it. He draped a friendly arm across Tag's shoulder, and it was like watching a horse trainer soothe a nervy colt. It probably didn't hurt that Dale and Tag had played Legion ball together, or that Tag bought his Sunday clothes at Dale's store. Dale was telling Tag how sorry he was about the wreck. He was sure it was an accident, he said, and he was sure they could work something out, something fair and square. Wylie kept expecting Maddy to say enough's enough—she hated Dale acting like he was her father—but tonight she seemed perfectly willing to sit back and let him clean up her mess.

There was nothing for Wylie to do except stand there look-ing useless. Once Tag cooled down, Dale actually convinced him and Maddy to shake hands. "That's it," he said. "Good sports. Both of you." By now the crowd was thinning out, disappointed no punches were thrown. Tag started back for his car, then stopped and gave Wylie a hurt look.

"And what do you got rolled up in that newspaper, brother?"

The last time Maddy won a race, three weeks earlier, she and Wylie had celebrated with a plate of vinegar fries, sitting on the hood of her car and joking about the skimpy prize money, how it would maybe buy a fan belt or an air filter for their dream car. Dale and Sheila were still up in the grand-stand, and Wylie'd had Maddy all to himself. Tonight, he hardly felt like he had her at all. She was sticking close to Dale. She said she hoped he didn't really plan on giving Tag any money to fix his car. Dale told her he'd worry about that later; right now all that mattered was that nobody got hurt.

The fender of Tag's Ford was bent into his rear tire. A couple of guys were helping him peel it back so he could at least tow the car home. Sheila went over to keep them com-pany, and Wylie decided to lend a hand. So what if it pissed Maddy off? He wanted to smooth things over before work tomorrow morning, and he was hoping that if the other drivers saw there was no bad blood between him and Tag, maybe they'd take it easy on Maddy next week, for his sake if not hers. He was about to fetch his crowbar from the truck when he noticed Kip Allen, the chief steward, talking with Maddy and Dale.

"You must be kidding," Maddy said.

Wylie walked over and asked what was going on, and Kip told him somebody had filed a protest. Maddy wouldn't get the win—or the winnings—until her car passed inspection.

"Who put up the teardown money?" Dale said.

Kip shrugged. "My guess would be Tag."

Dale looked disappointed. Tag was still squatting in the mud, but he and his pals had stopped pulling on the fender long enough to watch Kip deliver the news. They didn't try to hide their amusement.

Wylie was glad he hadn't made a fool of himself by going over to help. "Who ever heard of protesting a hobby race?"

"Not my idea," Kip said. "You can either break down the car, or you can forfeit. I get to go home sooner if you forfeit."

After Kip went back to his scut work, Wylie kicked the Ford's tire. "Shit. They can keep their fifty bucks."

"I am *not* forfeiting this race," Maddy said. "Damn it, I told you this would happen."

"You told me you wanted to win," Wylie said.

"Wait a second." Dale looked from Maddy to Wylie. "The car's not legit?"

After the last race, as the infield crowd was trickling out into the night, Maddy set the toolbox beside her car, popped the hood, and began tearing down the engine. It was almost eleven o'clock. Kip looked on, stifling a yawn. Sheila sat on the hood of the pickup with a beer, her legs dangling between the headlights, which were trained on Maddy's engine. A small group of onlookers had gathered. They were hobby drivers, mostly, and they'd stuck around to see Maddy get her due.

Across the track, Dale was smoking a cigarette in the empty grandstand. He wanted no part of this. He'd been peeved that Maddy never told him about the car, but mostly he just couldn't believe she planned to go through with the inspection. "Let me get this straight," he'd said. "You're willingly going to tear down the engine and *prove* you were cheating?" Maddy told him sometimes a person doesn't see what's right under his nose. She reminded him that if the car passed, she got to keep the fifty dollars for winning the race *plus* the hundred dollars teardown money. And anyway, she said, she had no choice: she had to call Tag's bluff.

"Tag's the one calling *your* bluff," Dale said.

"I'd forfeit, myself," Wylie said, "but it's up to the driver."

Dale had just walked off, shaking his head. Now he was watching the whole sorry scene from a comfortable distance, and Wylie wished he were, too. Maddy had his stomach in knots. Wrecking Tag had been a jackass thing to do, but at least he understood it. Not this stubbornness, though. She had to know the car would never pass, but she seemed to have talked herself into thinking it might, that she wouldn't have to forfeit *and* she wouldn't get nailed for cheating. That was Maddy: she couldn't help trying to have it both ways. Five more minutes and she'd have the engine apart, and everyone would know what they'd been up to, and then she'd turn to Dale to bail her out, and that would be the end of Wylie. Even a lugnut like Tag would know what to do if he were in Wylie's shoes: round up Sheila and hit the road before everything came crashing down.

But Wylie stayed put. It was one thing not to help tear down the engine, but he couldn't just leave her. By now she had the carburetor and the intake manifold off. One by one, the grandstand lights winked out until only the infield lights remained, swarms of moths orbiting the high poles. Except for the people who'd stuck around to watch, the place was empty, nothing but mud and trampled grass between Maddy's car and Tag's. He was leaning there with a beer. Maddy called over to him: "Getting your money's worth?"

"Don't look at me, sugar," Tag said. "I didn't put up no money."

A buzz went through the crowd. One guy, the driver who'd come in second place, was laughing and saying he *wished* he could take credit. His buddy mimicked Maddy in a slurry falsetto—"Getting your money's worth, Taggy?" Somebody else hollered for her to quit stalling. In the middle of all this, Sheila slid down off the truck. Wylie could barely make her out in the glare of the headlights, but he didn't need to see her face to know, sure as he was standing there, that she was the one who'd filed the protest. And from the look of it, she had some more business to take care of. She'd grabbed a couple beers and was weaving across the infield toward the gate, toward Dale, who apparently was about to hear the truth about his fiancée. Maddy seemed to have forgotten all about the car. She was biting her lip, following Sheila's progress as if she were watching a bad crash in slow motion. One of the head bolts slipped from her fingers and clanked down through the engine.

"Let's go, let's go." Kip tapped his micrometer against his leg, impatient for Maddy to get the cylinder head off so he could measure the bore. "I don't got all night."

Maddy didn't seem to hear him—she looked dazed— but she knelt in the wet grass anyway and began searching for the bolt in front of the tire, behind the tire, under the bumper. She'd been ignoring Wylie, determined to take apart the engine by herself, but under the circumstances, it was turning out to be more than she could handle. "Help me," she said.

Wylie watched Sheila as she crossed the track and disappeared into the shadow of the grandstand. Depending on what she knew, he still had a shot at convincing her there was nothing going on between him and Maddy. If that didn't work, he could always come clean and beg forgiveness—which was exactly what he could see Maddy doing with Dale. And who could blame her? Why put your faith in a guy like Wylie, a guy so bent on playing it safe that he had to wait for his girlfriend to blow the whistle? Right this second, Sheila was probably taking a seat next to Dale, bumming a smoke, offering him a beer. *You know, he's sleeping with her.* He could chase her down and fight for something he knew he didn't want; if it wasn't happiness, at least she'd never break his heart. Instead, he stooped beside Maddy and groped around in the darkness under the car. He didn't find the bolt, but he found her hand.

CHAPTER FIVE

1996

Holly

An hour or so before Lyle was fired for burning the most famous flag in America, Holly lost the last of their savings playing video poker on a machine likely owned by her father-in-law, Ellis Gandy, founder and president of Gandy Amusement. It was the end of May, and the heat had slammed into Columbia that morning like a wrecking ball. Lyle was at work at the statehouse. The building—subject of the master's thesis he'd failed to finish—was getting its first major face-lift in almost a century. The state had been too cheap to hire archaeologists to help with the excavation, so the task of unearthing artifacts had fallen to the workers. When Lyle's crew had discovered a buried trove of liquor bottles and discarded bones, he'd quickly fingered the corrupt Lincoln Republicans, who maintained a barroom right next to the senate chamber during Reconstruction.

"Apparently," Lyle told Holly at breakfast, "they were so lazy they just threw their garbage out the window."

Holly checked the kitchen clock. It was nearly half past eight. Normally Lyle was long gone by now, but here he was, helping himself to another cup of coffee, telling her how he'd managed to pocket two of the antique liquor bottles before

the guys from the state museum had arrived to tag the artifacts and trundle them away. To hear Lyle tell it, this wasn't
really stealing; he was the one who'd found the bottles, and
anyway, what good were they packed away in boxes at the
museum?

For all Holly cared, he could have stolen the statehouse
itself. Her only concern was being at the video parlor when
it opened at nine, but she had to wait until Lyle left or risk
him seeing her car parked at Fortunes on his way to work.
She glanced out the window. The last traces of fog hung low
and spotty over what had once been soybean fields. She
considered asking Lyle if he had any cash—for groceries,
she'd say. She was almost broke. No more money meant no
more poker.

"We counted the bones," Lyle was saying. "Pork was
their favorite."

"Aren't you going to be late?"

Lyle put down his coffee. "Don't you want to hear about
what we found?"

A week earlier, Holly had been the one suggesting they
might actually have a conversation at breakfast sometime.
Most mornings, if Lyle spoke at all, he spoke to the newspaper. He'd always been one to give *The State* a good talking-to,
and once upon a time, this had intrigued Holly—there was
something vaguely sexy about a man with political bones to
pick—but lately he muttered and swore at the news like it
was some kind of personal insult. All it took was a story about
the Confederate flag or the state's failed attempts to rid itself
of video poker, and boom, off he'd go.

"Sorry," Holly said. "I just thought you'd lost track of the
time."

"It's my job," he said. "Let me worry about it." The

implication being, he at least had a job to worry about. Not that he'd ever come out and say as much, but he'd said enough to turn Holly's face hot as she stole another glance at the clock.

That morning, she was supposed to be at the antique mall tending the booth she'd rented the previous summer, selling off the old farm implements and china she'd inherited when she inherited Cal's farm, but as usual, she stopped off first for a few hands of five-card draw. Fortunes Emporium was a converted cinder-block feed store that had been sub-divided into a warren of rooms housing five Pots-O-Gold each. At 8:50 a.m., there was a line out front waiting for the attendant, Billy Pecan, to unlock the door. These were the days when video poker ruled the state. Holly had read some-where that South Carolina had three times as many places to gamble as Nevada, and whenever she thought of her father-in-law, Ellis Gandy, one of the piedmont's chief suppliers of poker machines, it left her whipsawed. "Your dad must be making a mint," she'd said to Lyle more than once. But that's all she said. She had no business sounding like she wished Lyle were getting rich, too.

Years ago, before they'd met, Lyle had dropped out of graduate school and gone to work at Gandy Amusement, what was then his family's jukebox and pinball business, but on the day his father decided to add poker machines to their distribution routes, Lyle quit on the grounds that he didn't want to make a living off other people's misery. He hooked up with an outfit that renovated old homes and meanwhile launched a personal boycott, refusing to patronize any estab-lishment that housed a video-poker machine. By the time Holly married him, a few months after Cal died, Lyle had his own crew and was trying to make a go of it as a contractor.

Holly wanted to help, so she went back to school for a semester and took enough business courses to make herself useful as an office manager. While Lyle was out on the job, she manned the phone and fax machine in what used to be Cal's workshop, printing off invoices and purchase orders on their new laser printer. They spent weekends remodeling their own house, stripping woodwork, painting, tearing out old carpet, refinishing floors. Somewhere along the line, their modest projects gave way to more ambitious ones, and when they ran low on money, they reached for their stack of credit cards, thick as a poker deck. It was a familiar story, Holly supposed: You got a little and it only made you want more. Soon, everywhere they turned, they saw things they hadn't paid for: bathrooms done up in marble and sandstone, an HVAC system with enough BTUs for a polar bear, a kitchen straight out of *Southern Living*. It was around the time they decided to convert the attic into a master bedroom that Lyle's biggest client went belly up and business slowed down. To make matters worse, property taxes on the idle farmland were eating them alive. When Lyle got tired of struggling every week to make payroll, he closed up shop and took a construction job with plenty of overtime. Rather than get a real job herself, Holly leased the booth at the antique mall. They started seeing less of each other, and that started taking a toll.

Of course, the fact that they were going broke didn't keep Holly out of the video parlor. The more she lost, the worse she felt, and the worse she felt, the more she gambled. By the time Billy unlocked the door on that May morning, she'd gone through most of what was left of their savings, money Lyle had insisted they set aside for emergencies, a nest egg he'd managed not to disturb even when the credit card bills began to pile up. After she got change, Holly headed down the smoky hallway to a corner room where she found four other gamblers already nudged up to their touchscreens like cows at a feed carrel. Billy had put the OUT OF ORDER sign on her machine so nobody else would take it. She proceeded to chain-smoke and play five-card draw for three hours straight, hemorrhaging money at a buck twenty-five a hand, but it was a small price to pay. So long as she sat at that machine concentrating on straights and flushes and jackpots, she didn't have to think about the money she wasn't making at the antique mall, the house and all its half-finished projects, the expensive new mahogany bed where she and Lyle slept facing away from each other; she almost even managed not to think about their savings, the last fifty dollars of which now sat in a plastic bucket at her elbow.

By noon, Holly was down to five quarters, enough for one more hand. Anybody who plays video poker can tell you it messes with your head. You start out hoping to get rich, but before you know it, you've dug a hole so deep that it doesn't matter whether you're winning or losing; it's easier to keep digging than to climb back out. The most important thing—the only thing—is not to stop. Holly had seen old ladies win thousand-dollar jackpots and keep right on playing without batting an eye.

On her final hand, she found herself with a belly draw. Instead of the seven she needed, she drew a deuce. GAME OVER, the screen said. She blinked at the machine through a haze of cigarette smoke. Once, she'd seen a television show about AA in which they used the phrase "moment of clarity," and she waited for that now—waited to see herself in such a hard, bright light that she'd have no choice but to confront her so-called demons. But it didn't happen. All she could think about was getting caught, the hurt and disappointment on Lyle's face.

Naturally, she panicked. She had to win back the money. She rifled her pockets for stray bills and then stuck a finger into the coin-return slot, finding only a lump of chewing gum. Slipping from the stool, she searched the shag carpet, feeling for loose change and hatching wild plans to sell her old pickup and tell Lyle it had been stolen. How, she wondered, could this even be happening? When she looked up, Billy Pecan was hesitating in the doorway with a basket of popcorn. "You hungry, Holly?"

She stood up. The air felt thick as moss in her throat. "No, Billy, I'm broke."

He studied the popcorn. "You want a ride to the ATM?"

"I'm broke, Billy. I don't have any money to *get* from the ATM."

The steady electronic clicking of touchscreens ceased as the other players turned on their stools to look at Holly. All of them were regulars: Tim and Ray Fletcher, retired twins who cashed their army pension checks at the front counter each month; Janie Darling, a teller at Carolina First who should have known better; and of course Beatty Chapman, Lyle's foreman, who'd recently sunk so low that he pawned a diamond ring he'd inherited from his uncle, DeQuincy Arnold, the first black man elected to the state senate this century. For the past several months, this was the company she kept. They all took long lunches, told their spouses they had to work early or late, got caught in fictitious lines at the Winn-Dixie or the post office. Sooner or later, they all found a way to get to Fortunes. Now the four of them were looking at Holly the way two-legged people look at an amputee.

"Fine," Holly said. "Piss your life away, all of you. See if I care."

Janie sighed, a little impatient. "Here you go, honey," she said. "Now be a dear and let us piss ourselves in peace."

She was holding out a handful of quarters, five or six dollars, shiny new coins fresh from her drawer at the bank. Holly could feel the others watching her reflection on their screens, silently making odds, wishing she'd either take the money or leave, but as much as she wanted those quarters, she couldn't accept a handout in front of that crowd. She turned and hurried from the room, jarring loose the coins from Janie's hand and clipping Beatty's ashtray, sending an avalanche of ash onto his trousers.

Billy followed her all the way to the exit, where he stood holding the popcorn. "Holly, what time you coming back?"

Sooner or later, Lyle would find out. Holly understood this as she stood in the parking lot at Fortunes, letting hot air out of the cab. No use trying to hide it. She could either tell him the truth or wait, and she couldn't wait, because the waiting would be agony. Better to get it over with. In fact, she *wanted* to tell him, because once he saw how miserable and sorry she was, she knew he'd forgive her, and then she'd be out of trouble.

She fumbled through her glove box for a tissue and then pointed the pickup toward the statehouse. Lyle was too good for her, really. For more than a year now, he'd been patient and supportive while she played at being an antiques dealer, and instead of working harder or finding steady work or going back to school (she'd long since given up the idea of being a vet), she'd rewarded his faith by spending her days at Fortunes. And the money she'd lost had been more than just a nest egg; it had been insurance against the thing Lyle dreaded—having to go begging to his father.

As the football stadium and fairgrounds slid past, she kept telling herself this was all a blessing in disguise: If she hadn't lost their money, she wouldn't be ready to confess to Lyle, and if she didn't confess to Lyle, she'd never stop gambling. He'd probably suggest she see a psychologist, maybe give Gamblers Anonymous a try, and though she lacked his faith in professional help, she wouldn't object; she would do whatever it took to show him she wanted to get better. At the stoplights downtown, she bit her lip and tried to keep a steady hand. She was dripping Visine all over her cheeks.

When she parked on Main Street, Holly could hear the rumble of bulldozers and backhoes churning up what used to be the statehouse lawn. They'd started a forty-million-dollar renovation the previous fall, and now the project was well on its way to being a sixty-two-million-dollar albatross. Construction workers maneuvered dump trucks past bundles of rebar and mountains of sun-baked dirt. As she picked her way across the site, she saw Timothy Covey standing at the foot of the massive marble steps, staring up into the sky like he was waiting for some brain cells to fall down and hit him. When he wasn't blowing his paycheck at Fortunes, Covey worked on Beatty's crew with Lyle. Their job was to dig a trench around the statehouse and then retrofit the foundation with shock absorbers to protect against earthquakes. It was slow work. During the war, Sherman had burned the original blueprints, so now the crew had to creep along five feet at a time, never knowing what they'd find. At the base of the building, beneath the line of gray stone where the Caterpillar machines had bitten away the earth, red brick stood exposed for the first time in a hundred years.

"Have you seen Lyle?" Holly said.

When Covey didn't answer, she shaded her eyes to see what it was that had him so spellbound. The dome was cocooned in scaffolding except for the copper crown and the flagpole with its three flags—one for the United States, one for South Carolina, and one for the Confederacy. High against the sky, a lone worker was scaling the crown. Only when he began to shimmy up the flagpole did Holly understand something was wrong. The plans called for a major restoration of the dome. Eventually they were going to fix the leaks, restore the skylights, and replace all the copper plates, removing them to Charleston, where somebody with a lot of patience was going to make templates so each individual piece could be reproduced. According to a stipulation in the contract, all of this was to be done without disturbing the flags. But the man on the pole had other plans. From the look of it, he was now attempting to saw the Confederate battle flag in two with a pocketknife.

"Hey!" Covey yelled, shaking his fist at the sky. "Hey! Don't touch that flag!"

Holly had been hoping it wasn't Lyle up there, but of course it was, and of course she knew why: He intended to burn that flag.

Shortly after Holly had rented the booth at the antique mall, she and Lyle had found Cal's Confederate flag neatly folded inside a cedar chest atop a box of Christmas ornaments. Though they couldn't afford to finish the attic like they'd been planning to do, they'd been cleaning it out anyway, deciding what to keep and what to sell. She'd seen Rebel flags bring twenty dollars at flea markets, but before she could put it in the "sell" pile, Lyle suggested they burn it.

"Burn it?"

"Do you really want to make money off this thing?" he said, holding it out like a dirty sock.

It never would have occurred to Holly to destroy the flag, but the more she thought about it, the more she liked Lyle's idea. She kicked a box of old *Playboys*. "If we're going to burn the flag," she said, "we may as well burn these, too."

Soon they had a small pile in a clearing out behind the dairy building: the flag, Cal's magazines, a RE-ELECT STROM THURMOND button, an Aunt Jemima apron, a pincushion picturing a cartoonish black man with the word OUCH embroidered across the bottom, and the awful Hawaiian shirt Cal used to think made him look sporty. Lyle doused the pile with lighter fluid and Holly tossed a match on top. As smoke rose into the branches, the tree frogs and crickets began to trill. Holly and Lyle watched the flames cast shadows against the whitewashed concrete.

"Doesn't it make you feel good?" Lyle said. "Doesn't it make you feel clean?"

Holly was no sap. She knew that burning those things didn't make her a saint. At most, she and Lyle had made a modest sacrifice in the name of good taste. And to be honest, she wasn't sure she'd do it again; they could have used the money that stuff would have brought at the antique mall. Still, in a way, it *had* made her feel good. She'd married a man who stood up for what he believed in.

But this time, Lyle had gone too far, and Holly just didn't get it. Risking his life for a flag? This was how you got lynched in South Carolina; this was how you got pistol-whipped by the cops. She'd always figured that if the state wasn't smart enough to take it down, fine, whatever, let it fly—they all deserved the embarrassment. Now she watched in disbelief as Lyle finished cutting away a corner of the flag, slid down the pole, and disappeared into the honeycomb of scaffolding. It was like watching a stranger.

Somewhere somebody in a cement truck began to honk the horn, and Holly noticed several of the men had stopped working. They were dropping their shovels, pulling off heavy gloves, climbing down from bulldozers and cranes. They seemed to be migrating toward the east end of the building. Holly fell in behind three men who'd been breaking up some concrete with a jackhammer. She heard the shouting even before she made it around the corner. A tight knot of workers had gathered near the base of the scaffolding, beside a pile of seismic beams. Holly pushed her way through the crowd until she caught a glimpse of Lyle. He was down on one knee, T-shirt taut across his back, a slender curl of smoke already rising over his shoulder.

Holly got a shiver when Lyle stepped back and she saw the piece of flag on fire. No matter who you were, if you grew up in South Carolina, that flag was in your blood, love it or hate it. That winter at his desk, trying to ignore the pile of bills, Lyle had been writing letters to the editor of *The State,* blasting Governor Beasley for his support of the flag, demanding a voter referendum. The newspaper hadn't published any of them, and in March, Lyle had given up both his letter-writing campaign and his video-poker boycott. "What's the use?" he'd said. For Holly, this had been a relief, espe-

115

cially the end of the boycott. By then, almost a quarter of the state's retail businesses had video-poker machines, and she and Lyle had nearly run out of places to shoot pool, eat barbecue, and buy gas. Yes, she still had to listen to him cussing the newspaper, but she'd thought he was starting to lighten up a little. Until now.

Covey was trying to get at Lyle, but two bigger men were holding him with his arms pinned behind his back. "Fuck you!" Covey was saying. "That's the flag! That's our flag!" A faded tattoo of the very same flag peeked from beneath his sleeve. The veins bulged in his skinny arms and neck as he ranted about state heritage and the blood of his ancestors. Lyle just stood there. All Holly could figure was that her husband was drunk, or delirious from the heat. How else to explain it? When two site managers marched into the crowd and ordered everyone back to work, Lyle didn't even try to slip away. He caught sight of Holly as one of the managers stomped out the fire. He looked surprised, and a touch embarrassed, like the look he got when he smuggled home an old pickax or musket ball.

"Should I call a lawyer?" Holly said.

Lyle shook his head as the managers led him away. Holly felt a hand on her shoulder. "It's okay," Beatty said. "They won't want the police involved."

She watched as Lyle was ushered into the white trailer that served as the construction office. When the door clicked shut, Beatty removed his hard hat and hollered for everybody's attention.

"Okay, fellas," he said, passing the hat. "Time to pony up."

One by one, the workers began dropping cash into the hat. A collection for Lyle: Holly could hardly believe it. It was like a movie, like her husband was some kind of folk hero who'd done what everyone else only wished they had the guts to do.

The hat came back full of bills, mostly tens and twenties. Beatty dumped the money into a paper sack. "Give this to Lyle when you see him, sugar," he said, adding forty dollars from his own pocket as if it were an afterthought. He was wearing his diamond ring again. He'd managed to turn his luck.

Holly waited for Lyle outside the fence along Gervais Street. It had been almost fifteen minutes since they'd taken him into the trailer, and still there were no police, no reporters, no mob. Backhoes and bulldozers had resumed their work. Up on the dome, three men were already taking down the torn flag and putting up a new one. Holly couldn't hold out any longer. She opened the bag and peeked at the money. There must have been at least five hundred dollars. Two thousand quarters.

"I don't even want to know how much is in there," Lyle said. "I'm giving it all back." He was standing right beside her. She clinched the bag shut.

"Are you okay? What did they do to you?"

"Nothing," he said. "Fired me." He was smiling as if there were razors in his mouth and he was trying not to cut himself.

"You got yourself fired?" It hadn't occurred to Holly that he'd automatically lose his job. So that's why they'd passed the hat. She'd had some vague idea they were contributing to Lyle's legal fund.

"Don't worry, we'll be fine. What are you doing here, anyway?"

Holly considered telling him the truth, throwing it in his face. Maybe he wouldn't be standing there like such a dope if he knew about their savings. Maybe he'd wish he'd thought twice about losing his job. "Jesus Christ, Lyle. You could be in jail. You could have gotten killed."

"Yeah, well, I didn't," he said. "Don't make a big deal. You know how I feel about that flag."

"Lots of people don't like the flag."

"What was I supposed to do? Call and ask your permission?"

"Why didn't you say something this morning?"

"I didn't know this morning."

"Liar." Holly leaned in and sniffed. "Have you been drinking?"

"No," he said, "I've been working. Somebody's got to pay the bills."

Lyle caught Holly's wrist the first time she tried to slap him, but the second time, he shut his eyes and took it. For a moment they stood there as if some delicate artifact had dropped and shattered on the sidewalk between them. Lyle touched a finger to his cheek.

"What would you think," he said, "about me going back to work for my dad?"

Holly had read enough of Lyle's master's thesis to get the gist of it. He argued that compromise and mismanagement during the construction of the South Carolina statehouse had given rise to a building that did lasting damage to the state's self-esteem. When the original architect, John R. Niernsee, had drawn up plans in the 1850s, he had big things in mind. The capitol would be a fireproof repository for state records, built using only marble, iron, and granite; it would be crowned with a glorious 180-foot tower modeled on the Tennessee statehouse. But along came the war and Sherman, followed by a depression that nearly halted construction. After Niernsee died, the new architect ended up installing wooden floors and walls and substituting the less expensive dome for Niernsee's tower. It was, by all accounts, a half-assed job. A Washington architect hired to inspect the finished product declared it "a parody upon the science of architecture, an insult to the fame of John R. Niernsee, and a disgrace to the state of South Carolina."

Now Holly was sitting at a window in the Capitol Café, gazing across the street at the statehouse and listening to Lyle tell her that if he ever took another crack at his thesis, he'd do it differently. Compromise wasn't always a weakness, he said; sometimes it was a strength. "They got the thing built, didn't they?"

It was ninety-one degrees outside, and they'd come to the café under the pretense of cooling off, having a glass of iced tea, but really they just needed a quiet place where they could apologize to each other. Once they'd taken back the things they wished they hadn't said, Lyle told Holly he'd been thinking about quitting the statehouse all spring. As he began rambling about his thesis and the virtues of compromise, something clicked, and Holly finally understood his crusade against the video poker business: you fight the thing that pulls you hardest.

Lyle's father had been asking him to come back ever since he quit, and though Holly knew he was sick of being in debt, she still couldn't believe his change of heart. Was he doing it for her, because he thought it was what she wanted? *Was* it what she wanted? Yes, sure, there had definitely been times

when she'd resented Lyle for quitting Gandy, when she'd
wanted to ask him where he got off being so holier than thou.
Plenty of people had day jobs they weren't proud of. So
what? You did what you had to do. But now that she'd gone
behind his back and lost their savings, it wasn't so easy to
wish him into doing what made her life easier. The thought
of him coming home miserable from Gandy every night
wrung her insides.

"There's a difference between compromising and selling
out," Holly said. "I don't want you working for your father."

"Since when do you have something against video
poker?"

Behind him, three Pots-O-Gold stood along the back
wall. "I don't," she said, "but we're talking about you, not
me."

"He'll pay me three times what I was making at the
statehouse," Lyle said. "I thought you'd be happy."

"You know what made me happy? Watching you burn
that flag." It was half true, now that she considered it, but it
was also true she had no political qualms about her father-
in-law's line of work, because if people were dumb enough
to put all their money into a poker machine—herself
included—well, that was natural selection; that was how
the world maintained its quota of poor people. And somebody had to get rich off it, right?

Lyle couldn't help smiling. "I figured as long as I was
quitting, why not?" He ordered another iced tea and then,
cocking his head toward the video-poker machines, stood up
and motioned for Holly to bring the bag of money and join
him.

"So how do you play?" Lyle said.

The question caught Holly flat-footed, but Lyle didn't

notice. He was reading the rules, slipping five quarters into the slot. It was a multi-game Pot-O-Gold. He could take his pick from keno, bingo, blackjack, Shamrock Sevens, or Pieces of Eight Criss Cross, but he didn't hesitate in choosing five-card draw, Holly's bread and butter. That's when it hit her: he already knew all about her gambling. He was giving her a chance to come clean.

He dealt himself a hand. "These things are rigged, you know. The state doesn't regulate them."

Holly braced herself and began wending her way toward a confession. "That's why you have to find a loose one," she said. "Usually a new machine is best, especially if it's in some place that doesn't already have poker. They'll set the game so it's easy to win, to attract players, then later they'll switch it back."

Lyle paused in mid-draw. "Where'd you learn all that?"

And now Holly could tell from the look on his face that she'd been wrong. The possibility that she played poker had never crossed his mind. And further, she understood that she might not have to tell him at all: If he did go work for his father, they'd be rich; they'd never miss the money.

"You know that video parlor on Bluff Road?" she said. "Every once in a while, I like to stop in for a few hands."

"No kidding." Lyle studied her for a moment, and then he began to laugh, as if she'd just played some astounding trick on him and he couldn't help being impressed.

The next day—Holly's first as a reformed gambler and Lyle's first without a job—she flipped from one news broadcast to the next during breakfast, trying not to think about Fortunes and the jackpots everybody else was winning, trying instead to find a report about the flag so she could show Lyle he'd done something that mattered. After a while, she gave up and turned off the TV. Her heart wasn't in it. "Are you going to call your father?"

"In a while," he said, sliding the newspaper across the table. "Look at this." Sure enough, *The State* had come through—sort of. There was a story about Lyle on the front page of section B, but they didn't mention his name, and they didn't even speculate about why he'd burned the flag. The construction bosses were treating the whole episode as run-of-the-mill vandalism. The unidentified worker wasn't fired for desecrating the flag; he was fired for being in an area where he wasn't allowed, destroying property, and burning material on site. "It wouldn't have mattered to us if he had burned a two-by-four," the project manager was quoted as saying.

Holly said, "Shouldn't you go find a reporter or something? Tell your side of the story?"

"I wasn't trying to get on TV. Anyhow, they said they wouldn't file charges if I kept my mouth shut."

"For God's sake, Lyle, it's not like you robbed a bank."

Lyle took both of Holly's hands in his, just like he'd done the day he asked her to marry him, the day of her grandfather's funeral. Some people might have called it bad timing, but Lyle called it his way of balancing things out. That's what love was, he'd said—two people finding ways to balance each other against all the grief life slings your way.

"I know you're trying to make me feel better," he said, "but stop." He went out onto the porch in his bathrobe, carrying the two antique liquor bottles he'd brought home Wednesday. He'd already rinsed them, and now, settling on the steps, he went to work running a brush inside each one, loosening the last bits of dirt. Holly stood watching him at the window. The rest of his collection sat on a shelf in the den. They'd cleaned each piece—a section of the original copper cladding from the dome's cupola, a small pickax, two antique keys, a chunk of Tennessee marble, six roofing nails, one musket ball. She'd had her eye on an old oak display cabinet at the antique mall, thinking it would make a nice birthday gift for Lyle, but even before she'd figured a way to pay for it, he'd suggested they skip birthday presents this year to save money.

Holly arrived at the statehouse a little after one o'clock. She'd told Lyle she was going to the antique mall. She hadn't told him she intended to ask Beatty to rehire him. Lyle would have called it loyalty, maybe even love, but Holly knew, deep down, that she was only trying to make herself feel better. It occurred to her after breakfast, as she'd turned from the window and surveyed their living room—the three-thousand-dollar Italian leather sofa, the matching two-thousand-dollar chair, the space in between still waiting for a coffee table. Her not confessing to Lyle wasn't just about wanting to avoid his hurt and her shame. If she told him she'd lost their savings, it would confirm his worst fears about video poker. *His own wife.* And what if it scared him so badly that he changed his mind about working for his father? Holly wanted Lyle to be happy, and she certainly didn't want him to take the job on her account, but if he really was prepared to do it, she wasn't prepared to stop him.

So now she stood in front of the statehouse looking around for Beatty, all the while knowing full well it was pointless. They'd never take Lyle back. But she needed to be able to tell herself that she'd tried, that she'd done *something,* even if it was a lying-to-herself something that was really nothing.

She found a couple of workers from Beatty's crew eating lunch beneath a palmetto tree at the edge of the statehouse grounds. They told her Beatty had called in sick. *Sick of losing* was more like it. She drove back to Fortunes, refusing to think about the two fifties Lyle had given her for groceries, telling herself she wouldn't look at the jackpots, would not so much as sit at a machine. When she walked in, Billy Pecan was reheating a pot of coffee at the front counter. "Holly," he said, surprised. "I had to let somebody have your machine. It was getting late—"

"That's okay, Billy." She went down the hallway, checking each narrow room. Most of the regulars were there, including Timothy Covey, who was too busy dribbling Skoal into a Dixie cup to notice her. A few players did glance up, but, as usual, nobody said hello. They all pretended not to see each other, the way you'd act if you bumped into your pastor at a topless joint out in Cayce.

In the corner room, two pigtailed Girl Scouts were up on tiptoes playing Shamrock Sevens, coaxing a tinny Irish jig from the machine. Beatty was sitting beside them at Holly's Pot-O-Gold. Judging from his ashtray, he'd been there awhile.

"Oh, hey there, Holly, you want in here?" He'd just slid a twenty into the machine and dealt himself another hand of blackjack.

"Beatty, I need to talk to you."

"Not about Lyle, I hope."

"I think you should give him another chance."

"Shoot!" Beatty was busted with a twenty-two.

"Are you listening?"

"Now, sugar, I know, I know, I know. But I can't do it. Not my decision."

"He was only standing up for what he believes in."

"Please, Holly," Beatty said. "Look who you're talking to." He held up his hands, like maybe she'd never noticed the color of his skin. "You think I like that flag? But you don't see me burning it."

"Beatty," she said, "does your wife know you spend all day in here?"

Beatty drummed his fingers on his knee. His ring was missing again. "Look here," he said, "if that job was so important to Lyle, he wouldn't have done what he did. Simple as that. Nobody was twisting his arm. Anyway, he made out pretty good. Must have been, what, four hundred bucks in the kitty?"

"In the *kitty*?"

"You know—his take."

"You mean he was taking *bets* on burning the flag?"

Beatty turned back to the screen and drew a hand down his face, as if he wished he could erase his own mouth. "Gambling husband's better than a drinking husband," he said. "Anyhow, nobody thought he'd go through with it."

Holly found her way outside to the pay phone and lit a cigarette. So that's what burning the flag had been about— money. Or maybe it had been about principle, and the money was just gravy. What mattered was that Lyle hadn't been straight with her, but she couldn't manage to get worked up about that considering she hadn't been straight with him, either. Somehow they'd managed to balance things out. As she dug into her pocket for a quarter, she imagined him back at the house, shuffling around in his slippers and feeling ashamed for letting her think better of him than he deserved.

When he answered the phone, she told him she was at the video parlor on Bluff Road. She told him she'd been there every morning for months, during which time she'd lost several thousand dollars. "And I wasn't even going to tell you. Or I was maybe going to tell you, but only because I was scared you'd find out anyway, but now Beatty—did I mention Beatty's here?—he just said you burned the flag for money."

"My father's on the other line," Lyle said. "Can you hold on?"

"I want you to take the job. I just didn't want you to take it because of me."

"I know," he said. "Anyhow, I start on Monday. Now, don't hang up." He clicked over to finish the conversation with his father. When he came back, he told Holly to stay put. "I'll be there in five minutes," he said. "We'll celebrate."

Lyle arrived at Fortunes carrying the bag of cash he'd won from his coworkers. "We're either going to get back your money or go broke trying," he said. They found a pair of vacant machines in a room where two white-haired women sat sharing a bowl of peppermints. Lyle surprised Holly by handing each of the women a ten-dollar bill. "What goes around comes around," he said.

At first, playing poker alongside Lyle gave Holly the willies, but he kept peppering her with questions about rules and strategies as if this were a perfectly normal way for them to spend an afternoon. He didn't seem to notice that in the course of the last day, he had become exactly the person he never wanted to be. And only once or twice did Holly accuse herself of cowardice—selfish cowardice—because in fact it didn't really bother her. All in all, she was feeling pretty good about the way things had turned out. Each time she was hit by a pang—each time her stomach turned over and she felt sure that the giddy glow of their afternoon was about to wear off, that it would all seem hollow and sad— Lyle shoveled another bill into the machine, betraying no doubt or regret. As they began to lose money in earnest, they grinned at the irony of it and made jokes about patronizing the family business, investing in their future. If Lyle was faking it, Holly couldn't tell. A half hour later, when he hit a seven-hundred-dollar jackpot, she took it as a good omen.

The electronic cascade of bells had just ended when Covey poked his head in. "This must be the lucky room," he said. Then he saw Lyle and his smile withered into a frown. He peered around, like maybe he was hoping to find some cousins of his waiting in the wings, and then he was swinging at Lyle. Lyle saw it coming. He stepped aside as Covey's fist disappeared into the wall with a sickening crack.

"Fuck." Covey yanked his hand free in a cloud of plaster dust and together he and Lyle spun past Holly and the white-haired ladies, out into the hallway. Lyle caught Covey in a headlock, but somehow Covey managed to wriggle free. As he crabbed away from Lyle, he sniffled and ran a finger under his nose. That's when Holly realized he was crying. Tears were coming out of him like a baby. His knuckles were bleeding, but Holly could tell it wasn't pain making him cry. It was outrage—fury so strong, he couldn't do anything but cry. The idea of it blew her mind. Even if he did think the flag was more than a dumb piece of cloth—even if he truly bought into all of that blood-of-our-fathers business—still, was it worth it? By now Beatty was hurrying up the hallway from one end and Billy Pecan was coming from the other. As Holly stood there with a handful of money, watching the future vice president of Gandy Amusement close in on Covey, a small part of her wanted to cry, too, but even then, she knew the feeling would pass.

She grabbed Billy Pecan and held him back as Lyle cornered Covey against the change machine. "Show him, Lyle," she said. "Kick his cracker ass."

CHAPTER SIX

2001

Lyle

Some of the other kids are already doing addition, but Claire's having trouble with basic counting. One, two, three, four, six, five, sixteen, seventeen, eleventeen. Holly is convinced she's dyslexic. During the parent-teacher conference, Miss Peavy tells them not to worry, Claire's talking circles around her classmates, the numbers will come. But it's Holly's nature to worry. She took up smoking again when she was breast-feeding—maybe that's what did it. "She'll count when she's ready," Lyle says. "I didn't count till I was eighteen."

He's thirty-five now, Holly's thirty, and Claire's almost four, which means, according to the syndicated columnist in the paper, she'll soon begin forming permanent memories. "I don't want her first memory to be Mom sucking a Camel," Holly says. And on that point, Lyle agrees. They've worked hard to keep their habit a secret from Claire, going so far as to never utter the words "cigarette" or "smoke" in her presence. So it spooks them both, the following week, when Claire walks into the kitchen with a crayon dangling from her lip.

That night, they decide to quit together. Mathematically, it's a no-brainer. "Subtracting a negative is the same as adding," Holly says. "Adding is positive."

"And positive," Lyle says, "equals good."

Holly picks the day, a Saturday, because they'll both be home. "I'll need the moral support," she says—as if she's the only one quitting. Lyle lets it slide. She smokes a pack a day compared to his half pack, and she's been at it since high school whereas he didn't start until his twenties. Lyle intends to quit cold turkey, so he starts tapering off a week in advance. Holly, meanwhile, stockpiles prescriptions for nicotine gum and patches, asks around for a hypnotist, arranges to take the weekend off work, and starts smoking double time to make up for all the cigarettes she'll miss out on for the rest of her life.

On Friday, their last official day as smokers, Lyle comes home from work, where he's been negotiating a deal to distribute video poker machines in West Virginia now that they're illegal in South Carolina. He finds Holly and Claire on the kitchen floor, playing with wooden blocks. Claire is fidgeting. "What's two and two?" Holly says, moving pairs of blocks into a foursome. Claire looks away, pokes out her lip. Then, a huge smile. "A tutu! A tutu! Can I put on my tutu?" Holly says, "I give."

Once Claire is busy with her dress-up clothes—tutu, princess crown, elbow-length sequined gloves—Holly and Lyle slip out to their spot beside the rosebush, where they can keep an eye on her through the window. Holly kisses her cigarette before she lights it. "Little friend," she says, "your days are numbered. Your number's up. You can't argue with the numbers."

On average, nonsmokers outlive smokers by ten years. Holly has posted this bit of info on the fridge, for inspiration. They're determined to stick around long enough to see Claire graduate from college, get married or not, become whatever she becomes. Even so, quitting feels like a loss. In Lyle's memory, their early days are suffused with smoke, a gauzy cocoon holding them close. Cal hadn't approved, so they'd been secretive back then, too, indulging their vice behind the milk house, down by the bluff, up on the silo late at night.

"Would you still do that"—Lyle's flirting now—"share your last smoke with me?"

He's remembering when he first started working for Cal. It was his second day on the job, and during a break, he asked to bum a cigarette off Holly. He didn't really want to smoke, was just looking for an excuse to talk to her. "It's my last one," she told him. "But I'll share."

Now Holly gives him a curious look, hooks a finger in the pocket of his oxford. "Sucker," she says. "It wasn't really my last one." And then, before he has time to be surprised, she puts her other hand on his chest and kisses him hard, which is exactly what he'd been imagining that years-ago day as he passed the cigarette back to her.

"Hey!" Claire's tapping the window with a magic wand, her voice tinny behind the glass. "Too! Much! Kissing!" Holly says she'll be in soon and shakes loose another smoke as Lyle heads inside to start dinner. That's how it goes the rest of the evening, her ducking out while he brushes Claire's teeth, helps her into pajamas, reads to her in bed. Normally he and Holly do the whole routine together, but tonight he doesn't mind going it alone, especially not if the kiss was a preview of what's to come. It's been two months, two weeks, and four days; by now even Holly has to be getting the itch. But this is math they don't talk about. As Lyle lies in bed, watching a ball game and waiting, he tries not to get his hopes up. Probably the only reason she kissed him was the sudden memory of the old days, how much she wanted him back then. After a few innings, he gives up, turns off the TV, and goes downstairs. He's opening a bottle of wine when Holly comes through the screen door carrying spread-sheets.

"You coming to bed?"

"Soon," she says. "I'm enjoying my swan song."

"You know, they say nicotine kills your sex drive."

Holly opens a Diet Coke. "You know, they say the same about alcohol."

When Lyle nods off around eleven, drowsy from his fourth glass, she's still outside.

"Ouch," Holly said, shifting her weight on top of him. "Something's not right." She told him it felt like the equipment down there had been rearranged. Claire was four weeks old, and this was their first try since she was born. They were clumsy as teenagers, but in spite of the discomfort, Holly seemed happy afterward, pleased to know he still wanted her. After a couple weeks, though, it was as if she no longer needed to do it now that she'd proven to herself they still could. At first Lyle was patient. She'd feel sexier once she lost the extra pounds, once she stopped wetting herself every time she coughed, once it didn't hurt. Besides, her body was busy providing for Claire, and that was the important thing. But even after Holly quit nursing, even after he could once again put his tongue to her breast without feeling like a trespasser, even after whatever had been rearranged during labor got itself back to rights, still nothing.

Lyle took into consideration biology, was willing to allow for the possibility that what his body needed two or three times a week, hers now needed less often. But as the months wore on (the "once-a-months" was how he thought of them), he began to think Holly simply wasn't trying. If he pushed her, if he dropped enough hints, eventually she'd come around, but even that could take days. And then he was still left feeling not quite right, because he didn't just want sex, he wanted his wife to want him. When he brought it up, she was apologetic, then defensive.

"Look," she said. "I can't help it if I'm not in the mood. Do you want me just servicing you like a broken-down car?"

"No," he said. "Of course not." And he meant it. Sex as a favor was even more depressing than no sex at all.

Holly nudges Lyle with her elbow. It's Saturday morning, six-thirty. "I've been up since five," she says. "Can we have a smoke now?"

"Afraid not."

"Then there's not much reason to get up, is there?"

When Lyle ventures a hand on her thigh, she rolls over and blows her nose, probably trying to wake Claire. "I've been thinking," she says. "As long as we're at it, why don't we quit drinking, too?"

Lyle reaches into his briefs to adjust himself. What she means of course is that *he* should quit drinking. She stopped before she got pregnant, and now she hardly drinks at all. "We're quitting cigarettes because they kill you," he says. "Drinking a little bit doesn't."

"But you don't drink a little bit." She rolls over to scratch his back, a consolation prize. "And even when you do, you change. You're not you."

There's a knock on the bedroom door. Claire has a million excuses for venturing in before the hands of the clock point to seven and twelve. When Holly says, "Come in," she hops toward them, underpants on backward, both legs squeezed through one hole.

"My underwear is broken."

"What a coincidence," Lyle says. "I think your mom is broken, too."

Holly pats his cheek and sends him to make breakfast while she helps Claire get dressed. When they come into the kitchen, she tosses a pack of Camels onto the table. "Get these away from me, please."

The feel of the pack between his fingers is enough to make his lips tingle, and as he throws it away, he's already plotting to come back later, fish it out. "Hang tough," he says, handing Holly her coffee. "Don't puff." It's a saying he picked up the first time they quit, one that got on Holly's nerves, but he means it as a joke. He's hoping for a smile. Instead, over Claire's head, she shoots him a look so full of venom that Lyle at first thinks she must be kidding.

"You know," she says, slumping in her chair, "I was doing just fine."

Fine, she means, until he started back. Fine to the point that she could sit behind the register at the antique mall with smokers coming and going all around and not even be tempted. They'd both quit when they were trying for a baby, but then, around the time Claire turned one, Lyle lit up after a few too many beers at the office Christmas party. Soon he was smoking three or four a week. One night in

January, Holly followed him outside, drew a cigarette from his pack, and stared him down. "This is your fault," she said. "I asked you not to keep them around."

Now, as she sits across the table stewing, Lyle would like to remind her that he wasn't the one who put it in her mouth and lit it, but somehow he almost feels like he did. Later, when he's taking out the trash, he buries the pack of Camels under wet coffee grounds.

The morning smolders on. Lyle's skin feels like it's crawling with prickly-footed beetles. A massive vacuum yawns inside him. But every time he's ready to cave, he pictures himself wasting away in the hospital with lung cancer or standing at Holly's graveside while Claire weeps. He'd probably light up anyway if he had the chance, but he doesn't, because their plan is to stick together and stay busy. They weed the flower beds, take Claire to the zoo, buy a hot dog at Sandy's, and make their weekly pilgrimage to Winn-Dixie, where, when Claire isn't looking, they load up on licorice, jawbreakers, Cheez-Its, and Bubble Yum. Holly wears a nicotine patch and chews nicotine gum. She's so shaky she couldn't light a match if she tried. That night, instead of smoking, they get in bed with a box of Cheez-Its and crunch the numbers. Thirty smokes a day between them times 365 days = 10,950 smokes a year. Three dollars a pack times 10 packs a week times 56 weeks = $1,680 a year.

On Sunday, Holly switches over to licorice and Bubble Yum, and after another morning waging war on dandelions, they set out in search of the perfect jogging stroller, because now that they're taking care of themselves, they plan to start running. Holly won't shut up about smoking, though.

"Okay," she says, "is this little experiment over? Can we now resume our normal programming?" She's just trying to talk herself through it, but the talk grates on Lyle, because what he wants is to put smoking out of his mind, to forget, if only for a minute, that he's in constant want of something he can't have. Finally, standing in the stroller aisle at Babies "R" Us, trying to tell the difference between the $200 model and the $300 model, he asks her in the kindest voice he can manage to please, please give it a rest.

"Sure," she says, "as soon as you please, please give me an s-m-o-k-e."

The $300 stroller is still rattling around in Lyle's trunk on Monday afternoon when he stops at the flower shop in Five Points. They hadn't planned to spend so much, but it seemed to them, there in the store, that the higher the price, the stronger their commitment to quitting. Lyle buys a dozen gerbera daisies and a foil balloon with the word CON-GRATULATIONS! in cheery gold script. He'll surprise Holly at work; they'll celebrate making it through the weekend. Even so, it's hard to get excited about quitting when everyone else seems to think it's not worth the trouble. Walking back to his car, he passes no fewer than five smokers on the sidewalk, all of them seeming happy as clams. It's been like this all day, smokers everywhere he turns, as if the whole city is taunting him.

En route to the antique mall, he makes a point of driving past the statehouse to admire the gleaming copper dome. They took down the Confederate flag more than a year ago, but its absence still gives Lyle a good feeling, like the rest of the state has finally come around to his way of thinking. And

What You Have Left

who knows? Maybe one day they'll even ban smoking, and he and Holly can pat themselves on the back once again for having been ahead of their time. Never mind that the law-makers merely moved the flag to the statehouse lawn; like everything else, Lyle thinks, you measure progress one day at a time.

The antique mall is just down the hill from the state-house in the Vista, what was once the city's warehouse dis-trict. When Holly first rented a booth there, she'd just been piddling around, trying to sell off some of Cal's old junk. But after Lyle went back to work for his father and they had some extra cash, she started buying up vintage chandeliers, wall sconces, ceiling fixtures. She also tended the register now and then and eventually assumed the duties of manager. All the while, she was branching out into other areas of architectural salvage—doors, mantels, stained-glass windows, claw-foot tubs—which meant renting more and more space. Just before Claire turned two, the owner of the mall decided to retire. "We should buy it," Holly said as they lay in bed not having sex. "I'm renting half the place anyway, right?" Within weeks, she was the owner of Queen City Antiques, and Lyle found himself falling for her all over again, the way she paraded about the old warehouse rearranging showcases, chatting up customers, wooing dealers from other malls with promises of higher traffic and larger booths. Running a business was exhausting, though, and it was around this time that the once-a-months became once-every-other-months. Now, instead of not being in the mood, she was too worn out.

He parks beside the loading dock and checks the front desk, then the office. Finally he finds Holly trying to shoe-horn a marble-topped dresser between two armoires. "Hey, you," she says, glancing at the flowers with what looks like dismay.

Lyle drops the bouquet on a chair. "You didn't."

She gives the dresser another shove. It's still cockeyed.

"Well?" he says.

"Just one." Now she's trying not to smile. She always smiles when she's done something bad. Lyle's not amused. He spent the day grinding his molars, ready to gnaw off his own arm, and part of what pulled him through was the thought of her fighting the same fight.

"Where are they?"

The pack's right there in her pocket, and she's telling the truth: only one missing. Not that it matters. To the extent they're quitting as a team, they're back at square one, the whole weekend shot, and it's not just the disappointment that sacks Lyle, but the withering of his own resolve, the sense that *he's* now entitled to a smoke. He crumples the pack. "You suck."

"I know," she says. "I totally suck." But then she has the nerve to point out that it was only one cigarette, and one little cigarette isn't going to kill her. She tells him it made her dizzy, sick to her stomach. "That's a good sign, right? I didn't even want another one."

Lyle shakes his head and goes in search of Claire, trailing the balloon over his shoulder like smoke from a locomotive. After preschool, a sitter chaperones her as she toddles among the antiques, but the sitter's gone by now, which means Claire is probably over in the aisle with the replica Depression-era toys. Holly follows a few steps behind, still cajoling him, the way she might try coaxing a smile from Claire after a skinned knee. He wants to say something that will hurt—something less retarded than "You suck"—but it isn't until he sees Claire on the rocking horse that it comes to him. She's stroking the horse's neck, cooing in a voice so tender it splits his heart. "Balloon!" she says. Lyle scoops her up for a hug and turns to his wife, cuts her off.

"Look," he says. "It's simple. Either you do or you don't love your *daughter* enough to quit." In the next booth, two grandfather clocks begin to chime. Holly lowers her gaze to the floor, smoothes an eyebrow. Claire's asking her to look at the balloon, look what Dad brought, but she's having trouble putting on a sunny face.

In the days that follow, he has to give her credit. After he came down so hard, she could have sulked. She could have lashed out. She could have complained that he was drinking more than ever, that at night he was usually too drunk to follow along when she talked about commission fees or dealer contracts. Instead, she has rededicated herself to quitting. She goes back on the patch, even though it makes her queasy. She chews the gum, even though it tastes, she says, like burnt plastic. She hides a Hershey's kiss in the ashtray of his car with a note: *You light up my life.* On Friday afternoon, they take Claire jogging at the high school track. They're whipped after only two laps, but Holly seems proud of herself. She suggests they get a sitter, go out for a nice dinner. At the restaurant, they share a bottle of wine.

"Seven days and counting," she says, raising her glass.

"The week," Lyle says, "that lasted a year."

He's thinking this will be the night, but back at the house, after she slips out of her dress, she seems disappointed to find him in bed. It's a special occasion; she wants to celebrate. "One cigarette," she says. "We've been good. We deserve it."

He should have seen this coming. "But we're celebrating *not* smoking," he says. "Anyhow, if we get a pack, we'll smoke a pack."

"No, we won't." Holly has an idea. She tells him to go to the bar across the highway, buy a pack, take out two cigarettes, and give the rest away. "At a dollar-fifty apiece," she says, "we can't afford to get hooked."

Maybe it's the wine, or maybe it's just the curve of her hip in the lamplight, but at that moment, he doesn't have a better idea.

The place is called Benchwarmers, a shitty little sports bar that doubles as a bait shop during the day. Lyle's been doing business with the owner for years and has a soft spot for the old guy, who prefers pinball machines to video games and still leases a jukebox that plays 45s. Lyle's company owns the cigarette machine, too. It's against the back wall between bathrooms marked BAIT and TACKLE. Lyle buys a pack of Camels, removes two, and surveys the crowd. As usual, the bar is packed, plenty of smokers to choose from, but it's a tired-looking woman in a green evening gown who catches his eye. She's out of place—a refugee, maybe, from a wedding reception. She sits alone, nursing a Heineken. He didn't know they served Heineken.

"Want these?" he says. "I'm trying to quit."

The woman looks him over, skeptical, probably deciding if this is a pickup line, then slips the pack into her purse. "My lucky night," she says. "Thanks." He's already turning to leave when she clears her throat, nods toward a bar stool. "Sit?"

Lyle tries to keep a dumb grin from spreading all over

his face. He's forgotten how good it feels to be hit on. "I'd love to," he says, rolling the two cigarettes between his fingers, "but my wife's at home waiting for one of these."

Outside, he sits in his car, staring at the neon Pabst sign in the window, imagining himself back at the bar with the woman, having a drink. Of course his sex life isn't over at age thirty-five, not if he doesn't want it to be. But he's a decent man and he did the right thing, mentioning Holly right off, so that now, rather than enjoying the company of a woman who actually showed some interest, he's headed home to his frigid wife, where they'll proceed to wreck a week's worth of restraint and then, in all likelihood, not end up fooling around. Lyle has both cigarettes between his lips; they smell so good he could eat them. Instead, he flicks them out the window and drives another mile to the 7-Eleven, where he buys a pint of chocolate Häagen-Dazs. At the register, he picks up a Braves pocket schedule, the kind with a calendar inside. Holly's waiting for him on the porch.

"I got Häagen-Dazs," he says.

"Great." She opens the bag, glances inside. "Where's the smokes?"

"I changed my mind." He shrugs. "Tomorrow would just be that much harder, and it's already too hard as it is."

Holly assumes he's joking—she pats his shirt pocket to see if the cigarettes are hidden there—and then, realizing he's serious, she looks like she might haul off and hit him. "We had a deal," she says.

"Yes, we did. To stop smoking."

She clutches the bag and heads back inside. He figures she's going for her car keys, but when he catches up, she's shoveling ice cream into the kitchen sink with a wooden spoon. When she's done, she grabs a bottle from the wine rack—a decent cab he's been saving—uncorks it, and begins pouring it over the lumpy mounds. "You keep forgetting," she says. "This is a lot easier for you than it is for me." Maybe this is true, maybe not, but as he stares at the soupy mess, all he can think is how easy it would have been to take a seat on that bar stool.

The next morning, as Lyle is hanging the Braves schedule on the fridge and putting an X through each day since they quit, Holly announces that she's going out for a gallon of milk. This is the kind of errand she normally sends him on, so naturally he assumes she's sneaking off to cop a pack. Sure enough, when she gets home, she heads straight for the bathroom and washes her hands forever. But it doesn't stop there. Every night, she has a new errand to run—rent a movie, gas up the car, make a bank deposit—any excuse to get out of the house. She comes home smelling of spearmint gum, the door of her car flecked white with ashes.

Lyle wants to tell her he knows, but he's curious to see how long she'll keep it up. Meanwhile, he makes a point of marking the calendar when she's around. He asks how, on a scale of one to ten, she's holding up, whether the patch and gum are helping, whether she wants to call the hypnotist. He encourages Claire to play with the half-deflated celebratory balloon. He insists they go running, and once they're at the track, he pushes Holly to run faster, farther, pretending not to notice her sucking wind. At some point, it occurs to him he's being cruel—and dishonest—but every time he makes up his mind to say something, he puts it off, telling himself he's giving her the chance to come clean on her own.

"Here," he says, offering the pen. "Want to do the honors?"

It's Friday night, and Holly's just back from returning a video. Lyle searches her face for a flicker of guilt as she puts an X on the calendar. "Two weeks and counting," she says, reaching into the fridge for a leftover meatloaf. Lyle can't help glancing down the front of her shirt. What they really need is a calendar to track their drought. The streak now stands at three months, four days.

After dinner, they try to get Claire to practice counting, but she wants to do letters instead. She can bang through the alphabet in twelve seconds flat, "—now I know my ABCs, next time won't you tickle me." She loves to be tickled, so that's what they do. The three of them end up in a pile on the sofa. When Claire's had enough and scoots away, Lyle pulls Holly down for a kiss. "Stop!" she says, laughing. "You smell like a distillery."

"Are you saying you'd want to if I didn't?"

She squints at the blank TV screen. "No," she says. "I guess not."

He disentangles himself, stands up.

"Don't I get points for honesty?" she says.

"I think I'll go shoot some pool."

"Good idea," she says. "Why don't you have a few more drinks while you're at it? Maybe somebody else thinks that's sexy."

He sits at the bar with a Heineken, not minding the fog of secondhand smoke. But of course the woman in the green dress isn't there, and of course it's not a bar where he might otherwise hope to get lucky. A few women are standing around the pool tables, but they're with dates. The fact that he's chosen this place, he decides, must mean he doesn't really intend to cheat on his wife. On one hand, this is heartening, proof that there's hope for them. On the other hand, it means he's trapped. By now she's put Claire to bed and is probably on the porch, living it up.

After his fifth or sixth beer, Lyle asks Paul, the bartender, about the woman in the green dress. Paul knows exactly who he means. "Never seen her before, never seen her since."

"Too bad," Lyle says, pushing his empty across the bar. "One more, please."

The equation used to be so simple. Holly + Lyle = ♥. Corny, but true as anything he's ever known. Now the arithmetic is feeling more like algebra or trig or any of the other math he'd never quite got the hang of. Too many variables on either side of the equation. Her smoking cancels out his drinking. His drinking cancels out her disinterest. Her disinterest cancels out his being in this bar. The sum keeps getting closer to zero.

He's careful to drive the speed limit, careful to signal at every turn. Nearing downtown, he considers the lounge at the Marriott, but the chances of actually picking someone up are slim. He's already on Two Notch Road by the time he admits to himself what he's up to. He can see them here and there, on the corners, women in short skirts and tube tops who meet his gaze with a wave. He cruises the strip twice before spotting a slender girl in sandals and a white T-shirt loitering in the alcove of a laundromat. In the shadows, she looks younger than the others, less a professional. Lyle catches her eye, turns onto the next street, and watches as she hurries down the block. Cracking his window, he's surprised to find himself face to face with a woman not much younger than he is. Up close, she looks all out of proportion, her mouth too big for her face, her face too big for her head, her head too big for her body. She glances past him into the car, probably looking for handcuffs, a gun, another man crouched behind the seat.

"You the police?" she says.

"No."

"You *work* for the police?"

"No."

She winks at him, seeming for the first time like the girl he spotted in the alcove. "Then shut off those lights, baby."

Lyle does as he's told, and suddenly nothing about what he's doing seems safe. He's parked on a dark street in what was once a respectable neighborhood of modest four-squares, but now the houses are mostly boarded up, the yards dotted with trash. There are no streetlights. He considers driving away, but the woman is already climbing in beside him. The smell of coconut fills the car.

"I'm Denise," she says.

Lyle nods. "Nice to meet you."

She starts with the rules: money up front and nothing rough. "I don't play," she says, patting her purse. He's trying to decide if she might be carrying mace or a knife when suddenly she ducks. A car has turned onto the street behind them. Lyle can picture a police cruiser, the white glare of its spotlight. Then, as a rusty sedan slides by, he imagines a different scene, the tap of a pistol against his window, an angry demand for cash. He can't decide which would be worse.

"Relax, baby," Denise says. Her laughter is high and sweet, the laugh of a girl. She turns to him and asks what he's looking for, pointing first to her mouth, then to her crotch. "Twenty for this, forty for that."

"That," Lyle says. He feels ridiculous. She holds out her hand and he gives her two twenties.

"Well, baby, let's drive." She says she knows a place they can park—"a safe place"—and directs him down three or four streets, but they look no safer than the first street. Somewhere in the distance a car alarm is going off.

"Got a smoke?" she says.

"I wish."

She shrugs. "If wishes were dollars." She's wearing terry-cloth shorts. Lyle glances at her bare thighs. He can do this. If he gets laid, he'll at least feel like he's not completely at Holly's mercy. And if he gets laid, he'll probably feel bad enough about cheating not to do it again. One time is all it'll take. But his thoughts keep ricocheting like a pinball inside his head. What if she's leading him into an ambush? What if *she's* a cop? What if she has a disease?

"You've got a rubber, right?"

Denise shakes her head. "Don't worry. I'm clean."

Lyle tells her he can't do it without a condom.

"Okay, baby, no problem. Turn here."

They stop at a little service station with a CLOSED sign in the window. "Bathroom lock's busted," Denise says. "They got a machine." She's holding out her hand again. Lyle digs quarters from the console and drops them into her palm. Once she disappears around the corner, relief washes over him. He figures he's seen the last of her and his forty dollars, and it seems a small price to pay. But as he eases back onto the street, she comes running, waving and yelling for him to stop. "Where you going, baby?" Pulling away, he hears the sharp report of a quarter against his windshield and for a split second thinks he's been shot.

• • •

It's past one, and the house is dark. The car still reeks of coconut. He leaves the windows down and makes a mental note to get a car wash first thing in the morning. He's managed to unlock the kitchen door and is fumbling for the light switch when a silhouette looms over his shoulder. He spins around. His hands come up instinctively, ready to punch and pummel, then drop to his sides. In the loamy moonlight, Claire's balloon sways above a vent, the bulbous head of a clown. Lyle leans against the counter, adrenaline firing in his veins. He can feel his pulse in his hands, his face. He has to get hold of himself. He finds Holly's purse on the dining room table, the cigarettes in a zippered compartment beneath her compact. On the back porch, he smokes quickly, checking the bedroom window. By the fifth drag, he's light-headed and nauseous, and then he has to worry about how to hide the evidence. He ends up stubbing the cigarette out in the grass, then wrapping the butt in a paper towel and stuffing it into the kitchen garbage.

It isn't until he's lying in bed next to Holly, sleep overtaking him, that he realizes he should have flushed the cigarette down the toilet, and starts wondering if he really stubbed it all the way out. After a while, he's convinced he smells smoke. He's convinced he can hear the crackle of flames. But this is just his imagination, because if he were really hearing the crackle of flames, he'd also be hearing the smoke detector in the kitchen. Assuming it works. Assuming the battery isn't dead. Didn't he replace the battery a few months ago? Or did he just remove the old one when the alarm began to chirp? Again and again, he drags himself from bed and sloughs downstairs to peer into the garbage, only to wake and find himself still in bed, half dreaming. And then, when he finally manages to drift off, the house does catch fire, choking black smoke everywhere, Claire screaming for help.

"Bad dream?"

It's morning. The sheets are damp with sweat. Holly's leaning in the doorway, arms crossed.

"The house was on fire," he says.

"God forbid." She comes over and takes a seat on the bed. Only then does he notice the pack of cigarettes in her hand. In his rush to hide the butt, he'd forgotten about the pack, left it in plain sight on the table. Holly looks at him looking at the cigarettes.

"I found them in your purse," he says.

"I haven't quit."

"I know."

She stretches out beside him, and for a while they just lie there, shoulder to shoulder, staring up at the uneven plaster, the twinkly chandelier they spent months picking out. "So," she says, "any luck last night?"

Lyle closes his eyes. He can still see the house blazing, can still hear Claire's cries. He starts to tell a lie about spending the night losing his shirt at pool, then gives up.

"I almost fucked a hooker."

Holly props herself up on an elbow to see if he's telling the truth. She almost looks impressed. "How about that." She goes to the window and stares out at their front yard. "But you didn't."

"No."

She's still got her back to him, but he can imagine the concentration in her eyes, the weighty computations she's wrestling with. "I guess that's not so bad," she says, turning

150

around. "I mean, I don't have to throw you out. I don't have to divorce you."

What freezes Lyle is her robe hanging open. She stands like that beside the window with the morning light on her skin, luminous as ivory, staring hard at him until he has to look down, away from her eyes, but her breasts are shaming him, too, and her unblinking navel, and the sunlit patch of hair below. He can feel the weight of her against him all the way across the room. She's cinching the robe before he remembers to inhale again.

CHAPTER SEVEN

1979

Wylie

When Wylie doesn't see Tracy Evans's car in front of the boutique, he figures he's already missed her; he's driven all the way to Pawleys Island this morning for nothing. He picked up the packet of custody papers from the Myrtle Beach clerk of courts weeks ago, and this is what he gets for putting it off. By now, Ms. Evans and her 280ZX are probably halfway to Columbia, part of the migration inland, fleeing the hurricane.

The boutique is just off Highway 17 in what used to be a general store—a whitewashed building whose raised-seam roof and sloping porch have been painted a cheery orange. Out front, where crushed shells give way to scrub grass, there are rocking chairs, two joggling boards, hammocks strung between live oaks. It's no surprise the place is almost deserted. People aren't buying saltwater taffy and polished seashells today; they want flashlights, bottled water, batteries, canned goods.

Wylie parks in the shade between the only other cars, neither of them Tracy's Datsun. He half hopes she's long gone. In the four months he's worked as a process server, this is the lousiest job yet, worse than the restraining orders, the divorces, the cease-and-desists. Custody papers. How perfect is that, considering Wylie hasn't laid eyes on his own kid in more than three years? He dropped Holly off at Cal's farm the day after Maddy's funeral, and now that he's finally back on his feet, back to where he could be a father again, the old man won't give him a break. Cal's way of thinking is that people can't change. Well, they do change, just like circumstances change. One day your wife is alive, the next day she's dead from a blood clot. And for the Wylie of three years ago, Maddy's death had been like an opening, an unexpected tear in the cloth of his life. He'd simply let himself slip through. Didn't plan it that way, but so it goes.

That's Hugh's phrase, Hugh the lawyer Wylie works for. So it goes, my friend, so it goes. Of course, that's easy for Hugh to say. He's never been a father; he's never had to deal with a father-in-law like Cal. To Hugh, a custody case is the same as any other—a cash cow waiting to be milked. The thing about this case, though, is the cow's not in the barn. Hugh called Wylie this morning to remind him that midnight is the deadline for good service. If Wylie doesn't find Tracy Evans by then, the hearing will have to be rescheduled. Hence, thus, and therefore, he has to track her down today and deliver the return-of-service to Hugh this afternoon, at the pier in Garden City.

The last thing Wylie wants to do now is drive the twenty-five miles back to Tracy's house in Myrtle Beach— a wild goose chase—but it's no use wasting time on a stake-out if she isn't even coming to work. From where he's parked, he can see a dumpster peeking around the back corner of the building, but no Datsun. Still, it's possible she's inside—maybe she got a ride to work, maybe her car's in the shop. At this point, he's got no choice but to make like the wolf in grandma's clothes, stroll in there with a big, friendly smile, and try his luck.

Which he will, just as soon as he hears a weather report. Hurricane David is supposed to make landfall tonight, maybe the biggest storm in twenty years. Eight hundred Dominicans dead in its wake, the coast of Florida like a parade nobody cleaned up after. They've already started evacuating the barrier islands, setting up shelters in every church and gymnasium between here and Savannah. Wylie's trying to tune in a station out of Charleston, thinking about the damage the next twenty-four hours will bring—thank Christ he won't be the one who'll have to settle all those claims—when he glances up and sees something that makes him forget all about the storm. A boy has come out of the shop, maybe ten or eleven years old, carrying a wooden crate. Right off, Wylie knows it's Tracy's kid, the boy she's going to lose. As if serving papers on the mother wasn't enough, now he gets to do it while the son watches.

Hugh had promised that the kid would be out of the picture this week, staying with his dad. It doesn't look like he's staying with his dad. It looks like he's come outside to do a chore for his mother—unhook the hammocks and pile them in the crate. Wylie has half a mind to leave. If it weren't for the money, he would. But he needs the thirty bucks. Every penny is one penny closer to getting out of the By the Sea Motel and into an apartment where he won't be ashamed to bring his daughter. So he slips quietly from the car and cuts through the grass, hoping to avoid the boy. But just as he reaches the porch, the kid spins around, startled, as if Wylie has materialized from thin air.

"You must be Ted," Wylie says. It never hurts to be sure. He tries for a neighborly smile, would offer his hand if he thought he could keep it steady.

"Yes, sir?" The boy studies his face. Wylie knows it's not a pretty sight, what he's done to himself these past few years. After the funeral, when he left Holly, he'd meant to be gone only a couple of days, a little time to figure things out. He didn't plan on staying gone. He was only a few years shy of making district claims manager at State Farm, was already saving for the down payment on a nice little house in Forest Acres with room in the driveway for a bass boat, maybe a deck out back. You don't plan to ditch a life like that. But two months later found him in Atlanta, passing afternoons in the cheap seats at Fulton County Stadium. Another month and he'd begun a string of jobs that were easy to get, easy to leave—tending bar in Bamberg, pumping gas at a Beaufort marina, driving a mill truck out of Greenville. What he did mostly, though, was drink, every single day for almost three years, a stretch of time that bends and ripples in his memory, as if seen underwater, or through a glass. In the end, it took a DUI and ninety days in the Horry County Jail to dry him out; if he still looks like a drunk stumbling off the highway, so it goes.

"School out for the hurricane?"

Ted nods.

Wylie glances at the store. He's close enough now to see three women watching from the window. "Last I heard, they're saying the storm's out of gas."

Ted shakes his head. "It is not."

Wylie shades his eyes. Up and down the highway, it's sunny skies, the South Carolina you know from postcards. "What makes you so sure?"

"My mom," Ted says. "She saw the Gray Man."

"Who's that?" Wylie says, though he already knows. When he was Ted's age, his grandmother used to sit on the dock behind their beach cottage, plying him with ghost stories so long as he kept her paper cup three fingers full of sherry. He must have heard the legend of the Gray Man a hundred times.

"Don't you know?" Ted says, lowering his voice like they're sitting around a campfire. "The ghost."

And Wylie can't resist. "Tell me the story?"

"It's not a story," Ted says. "It's true." He takes his time getting settled on one of the joggling boards, clearly glad for a break from his chores. "What happened was, once upon a time, there was this man—he lived on Pawleys Island—this was back when people rode horses instead of cars. And he was going to see his girlfriend. He was going to ask her to marry him." Ted smirks at this. "But his horse wasn't watching where he was going, and he stepped in quicksand, and they both got swallowed up and died."

"That must have broken the girlfriend's heart." Wylie takes a seat on the other end of the joggling board, and the boy automatically starts it bouncing.

"It did," Ted says. "She spent the whole next day crying and walking on the beach all by herself. And that's when she saw the man. Only he wasn't a normal man. He was all gray."

"Her boyfriend?"

Ted nods impatiently—*of course.* "But when she reached out to touch him, her hand went right through and then he just turned into a puff of fog." That night, Ted says, the girl dreamed she was in a boat in the middle of the ocean during a terrible storm. It scared her so much, she made her whole family leave the island the next morning. "They thought she was crazy"—Ted twirls a finger around his ear—"but then a hurricane came and killed everybody on the island. They all drowned. The crabs and sharks ate their guts."

"Mmm," Wylie says, rubbing his stomach. "Pickled people."

It takes Ted a moment to stop giggling and get back to his campfire voice. "Now the Gray Man walks up and down the beach whenever there's a storm. He comes to warn everybody who's smart enough to listen."

"To warn everybody?" Wylie says. "I always figured he was coming back to look for what he'd lost."

The joggling board comes to a stop. "I thought you never heard of him."

Wylie manages a smile. Right now, *he* could use a cup of sherry. "You know, maybe I did hear it once." But when he winks at the boy, all he gets is a flat stare.

"Actually," Wylie says, checking his watch, "I'm here to see your mother. She around?"

Inside the boutique, three women are speaking in low voices at the register. They stop talking and beam bright smiles at Wylie as he comes in. Any of them could be Ted's mother. A blonde, a brunette, and a redhead—like Neapolitan ice cream, Wylie thinks. Quarts of it have taken the place of vodka in his icebox. The brunette sets down her mug and comes out from behind the counter. "Can I help you?"

She has a swagger not unlike Maddy's—a woman who knows how long her legs are—and Wylie is surprised to think he was married to a woman like that. That a woman like that would have been married to *him*. When he thinks of her, the picture he always gets is from a spring night in 1972, the two of them taking turns pushing a stroller down a dusty lane on Cal's farm, praying dear God for the baby to stop howling and fall asleep. Maddy sauntering along in a halter top and short-shorts, sipping High Life from a bottle she kept tucked in the baby's blanket, him thinking she looked too good to be pushing a stroller.

"I'm here to see Tracy Evans," he says.

A look passes among the women, a crisscross of glances too quick for Wylie to untangle. Hugh had promised that Tracy wasn't expecting the summons, but it's clear they're on to him. The brunette tucks a stray curl behind her ear, picks an imaginary bit of lint from the sleeve of her yellow blouse. "Tracy's out buying tape for the windows."

She may as well have said, *There, I'm lying. What are you going to do?* Which is par for the course. In the past few months, Wylie has been cursed, threatened, even spit on.

"The boy said she was here."

"That kid's in his own world," she says. "If you ask me, his mom lets him play too much of that—what's it called?"

"Dungeons and Dragons," says the redhead.

"I've been asked to deliver some papers. If it's no trouble, I'll just wait."

"Papers?" the brunette says.

Wylie clears his throat. "Legal documents."

"You mean custody papers."

"I don't read them," Wylie says. "I just deliver them." Which is bullshit, of course. And anyway, what the documents don't tell him, Hugh does. Wylie knows that Tracy's ex-husband is Boyd Evans, the developer, a man who's made his mint off blue-hairs from New Jersey, a builder of expensive oceanfront condos, proof you can't buy good taste. In the year since the divorce, Ted has been living with Tracy, but now that Boyd is remarrying, he wants his son. To hear Hugh tell it, Tracy doesn't stand a chance.

"If you say so," she says. "Now, if you'll excuse me, I've got work to do."

Judging from the silence that settles over the boutique as the brunette slips out the door, Wylie would bet the ranch that she's the one he wants. The redhead busies herself rearranging knickknacks on a shelf—coral paperweights, necklaces made of seashells, sand dollars painted to look like cats. "Hey, Barb," she says. "Why don't you get us a weather report?"

"In a sec." Barb the Blonde is dropping strawberries and ice cubes into a blender. Frozen daiquiris, at eleven in the morning. That's what a hurricane will do for you, Wylie thinks—it'll turn a Tuesday into a holiday. Folks are either running for their lives or throwing a party. He goes to the window to make sure Tracy isn't headed for one of the cars. To his relief, she's staying put just beyond the porch, helping Ted load the last of the hammocks into the crate. And if he had any lingering doubt that this was in fact Tracy Evans, it's gone now; anyone with two eyes could see that she and the boy belong together.

The redhead strolls over to the television and flips through the channels as Barb tops off the blender with a healthy pour of rum. Wylie can smell the sweet bite of it all the way across the room. What he wouldn't do for one quick pull from that bottle.

"I know that's Tracy out there," he says. "And I know she's your friend. But the judge is going to call this obstruction of justice."

"Shh," Red says, adjusting the TV volume as Barb clicks

off the blender. Even Wylie turns to watch. For once, the lead story isn't inflation or the arms treaty; it's Hurricane David—shots of military police on standby in Florence, yachtsmen at Kiawah towing their boats out of the water. A man from the Department of Wildlife and Marine Resources tells a reporter that the flooding may cause snakes and alligators to be uprooted from their natural habitats. *They're liable to turn up anywhere—your yard, your house, your swimming pool.*

"Did you know," Barb says, "that this is the first year they've named hurricanes after men?"

"About time," says Red, smiling at Wylie as she opens the door for Ted and his mother. They're coming up the steps with the crate, which they angle through the doorway and carry toward the back of the shop.

"Stick these in here?" Tracy asks as they disappear into the storeroom.

Barb nods, then points a crumpled pack of Salems in Wylie's direction. "Smoke?"

"No, thanks."

"I know, nasty habit." She lights up, shakes the match out with a soft laugh. "I'll quit as soon as I learn two things: how they make 'em so good, and how they make 'em so cheap."

But Wylie isn't listening. He's already past both women, on his way to the storeroom.

"Hold on," Barb says. "You can't go in there."

When Wylie opens the door, the room is deserted, no sign of Tracy or Ted except for the overturned crate and its coils of rope. Then he hears a car. He follows the sound through the back door, out into the blustery afternoon. Sure enough, it's the 280ZX, hidden between the dumpster and a wilted row of wax myrtles. Tracy nearly clips him as she backs out.

It's not until then, as he steps aside to let the car pass—as he sees the boxes and suitcases piled in the hatchback—that it dawns on him: Rather than risk losing her son in court, Tracy is kidnapping him, has been planning to all along. And what better cover than a hurricane? What better lie to tell the kid? It's just dumb luck he caught her at the boutique, maybe picking up her last paycheck, borrowing some extra cash, saying good-bye.

Wylie hurries around the building in time to see her turn north onto the highway. In the past four months, he's yet to fail at delivering a packet, and he doesn't intend to start today. As he climbs into his car, Tracy's friends come out onto the porch and stand at the rail, drinks in hand, not quite smiling. They look at him like they know everything—not just about his sleazy job, but also the daughter he left, the dead wife whose grave he doesn't visit. They're looking at him like he gets what he deserves.

Wylie catches up with Tracy at a stoplight just south of Myrtle Beach and follows her for about a mile, until she pulls into Coastal Federal Savings. Aside from the gas stations and the Winn-Dixie, the bank is the only place in town doing any business, people getting money for the road, not knowing what they'll find when they return: flattened homes, washed-out bridges, power lines writhing like tentacles in the streets. But if Wylie's right, Tracy won't be coming back. She's here to empty her account. Getaway cash.

By the time he finds a parking space, she's already heading across the lot, moving like there's no time to lose. Wylie doesn't like having been tricked, made a fool of, and as he watches her sidestep a scuttling windblown can, he has to keep reminding himself: Here's a woman taking a big risk, giving up everything for her kid—no more alimony, no more country club, no more fancy house on the marsh. How can he be angry? In fact, he's rooting for her. Because, really, they're in the same boat. For a moment he even allows himself to imagine them ditching the Datsun together, stopping in Columbia for Holly (*Sorry, Cal, step aside*), then heading up I-77—two parents on the lam with their kids, trying to salvage what's left of their lives.

Once Tracy is inside, Wylie approaches the car, careful that the boy doesn't see him. He wants to be sure he doesn't give Tracy another chance to make this harder than it already is. Ted is leafing through a stack of comic books and drinking a Tab. Wylie can't imagine how Tracy has explained to Ted what happened back at the boutique—assuming the boy believes they're just running from the hurricane—but no doubt Wylie gets tagged as the villain. Which is perfectly understandable, but still he feels bad about the way things turned out with Ted, because he thought they'd hit it off pretty good—a lot better than he usually does with kids. Usually they're scared of him. He can see it in their eyes when he smiles at them in line at Eckerd's, when he stops to admire their sandcastles on the beach. Just yesterday, at the post office mailing cash to Holly, he'd knelt down to pick up a little girl's Slinky from the floor and she'd refused to take it from his jitterbug hand. Now he wishes he had some candy in his pocket, wishes he knew even one Princess Leia joke that wasn't X-rated—anything to show the kid he's not so bad.

He's still standing behind the Datsun, trying not to attract attention, when Ted spots him in the side mirror. Immediately the boy lays on the horn. And doesn't let up.

It's so loud you'd think someone was robbing the bank. Across the street, two men boarding a storefront turn to watch as Wylie raps on Ted's window, trying to get him to knock it off. But he doesn't stop until Tracy comes running out of the bank, yelling at Wylie across the roof of the car. "How dare you!"

Wylie steps back, raises both hands like he would in a holdup. *Easy, now.* "For God's sake. Will you just take the papers?"

"I know the law," she says. "You have to put them in my hand."

Dodging service is illegal, but Wylie doesn't waste his breath. He makes a dash around the car. Tracy is too quick, though, and it turns into a one-lap footrace that ends with them back on their original sides. As Ted reaches over and unlocks her door, she gives Wylie a little snakebite of a smile and climbs in, disappearing behind the reflection of dark clouds on the windshield.

Tracy is halfway out of the parking space when she hits the brakes so hard the tires chirp. Wylie looks over his shoulder and sees why. A cruiser is coming around the corner of the bank, headed their way. If she really is running off with the boy, her ex may be on to her by now, in which case the police may be looking for her car. The cruiser slows as it passes the Datsun, swerving to avoid its bumper. Wylie thinks he sees the officer checking Tracy's plates, reaching for his radio.

He watches the cruiser park farther down the row. By now Tracy has pulled back into her space. She has both hands on the wheel, eyes straight ahead, and Wylie knows she's thinking this is it—this is where she gets busted. Or where Wylie turns her in. And he *should* turn her in, he's got every right, but if she would just listen to him for a minute, he'd tell her to relax. The only thing he cares about is delivering the papers. What she does with them is her business.

The cop is a grim fireplug of a man, uniform tight as a sandbag. He looks like a guy with a hurricane on his mind, a guy who, like Wylie, would rather eat nails than get mixed up in a custody fight. When he reaches the Datsun, he gives the three of them a lingering sidelong glance from beneath the brim of his hat and keeps right on walking. He's not looking for Tracy after all. But it's clear he senses something here. A situation.

At the entrance to the bank, he swivels back around and squints, all neck and shoulders. And even though Tracy is the one breaking the law, Wylie can't help feeling like *he's* in trouble—the sight of a cop still does it to him every time. To keep his hands busy, he pretends to search his pockets for a key, even as he realizes this is a ridiculous thing to do, because if he belonged in the car, wouldn't the woman just unlock the door? But by now the officer has lost interest. He turns away, maybe figuring they're just a husband and wife having a spat. He won't get involved unless somebody asks him to.

When the cop is inside, Tracy reaches across the car and rolls down the window. Wylie is relieved for the chance to explain, but Tracy doesn't let him. "Okay, you son of a bitch," she says, opening her purse and pulling out her wallet. "Is this enough?"

Wylie glances at the money, expecting a ten or a twenty—a bribe he doesn't intend to take—but what he sees is four fifties. More than six times what he'll make for this job. Half a month's rent on an apartment. Enough that he *could* afford to just let her go, tell Hugh she skipped town. But he can't get past the way Tracy is looking at him as she holds out the money. Not like she wants to spit on him, but like he himself *is* spit. And he wants to wipe that look right off her face, because he's been a good sport up to now, and besides, she doesn't know the first thing about him, the position he's in. If people assume the worst of you, then that's what they should get. Taking her money isn't even enough. As he reaches for the bills, he can feel himself giving in to his meanest instincts. And just like it is with everything else, he can't stop.

"I'm not the one kidnapping my son," he says, slipping the money into his pocket. "Have you bothered telling him he'll never see his father again?"

Then, for good measure, he reaches across Ted and drops the service package onto Tracy's lap. She's too stunned to stop the papers as they slide to the floor. What Wylie's not expecting is the kid's skinny elbow, the pointy snap of it right in his eye. He sees it coming too late, feels bone on bone like someone has sloshed a bucket of pain in his face.

"Liar!" Ted shouts.

It's all Wylie can do to get his arm out of the car before the window catches his elbow. He staggers away, half of the parking lot going dim and watery as the service package comes flying back at him, a spray of papers in the wind.

The hurricane party is in full swing by the time Wylie reaches Garden City. From the sandy path alongside the pavilion, he can see people out on the pier, hear music echoing across the waves. Farther down the beach, some kids with surfboards are bobbing in the swells as two policemen try to wave them ashore. Through his good eye, Wylie watches the officers advance and retreat with the surf, thinking it's not too late to turn Tracy in, give them her license plate number, tell them the son of a prominent citizen has been abducted. Why should she get to ride off into the sunset with Ted while he's stuck here with nothing but two hundred bucks and a black eye? To hell with that, Wylie thinks. To hell with sitting here on his hands. Tracy Evans isn't the only one who can do right by her kid. If he skips the party and leaves the return-of-service in Hugh's car, he can be on the road before the hurricane hits. Traffic willing, he'll reach Columbia by nightfall.

On the entrance to the pavilion, there's a hand-lettered sign—CLOSED FOR HURRICANE—but the door is unlocked. Inside, Wylie picks his way among dark pool tables and skee ball games. Behind the deserted bar, he wraps a handful of ice in a dishrag he finds draped over the tap. The pay phone is in the corner. Holding the ice pack to his face, he dials Cal's number. Holly answers on the third ring.

"Hampton residence," she says. "This is Holly."

Wylie has to pull up a stool, sit down. It's the first time he's heard her voice in more than a year. He used to call once a week. And he's always provided for her—turned everything over to Cal and still sends cash every month. But last year, on the second anniversary of Maddy's death, Cal read him the riot act. "I believe you care about your girl, Wylie," Cal said. "Problem is, you don't care enough." After that, when Wylie called, Cal just hung up. Didn't even give him a chance.

Now Holly sounds so grown up, self-assured, the kind of kid who orders for herself in restaurants, who could sell you a whole case of Girl Scout cookies on the morning you look in the mirror and swear off sweets for good.

"Hello?" she says.

The phone is shaking in Wylie's hand. He fumbles with

the ice pack, switches ears. In the background, he hears Cal asking, "Who is it?," then the muffled sound of the phone changing hands.

"Who's there?" Cal says.

Wylie tries a few lines in his head. *Pack her things, Cal. I'm on my way.* He's had it with Cal acting as if Maddy gazed down from the heavens and told him *he* was in charge. She was as much his wife as she was Cal's daughter.

"I can hear you breathing," Cal says. "You're not fooling anybody."

Now it's Holly in the background: "Is it a pervert?"

Wylie closes his eyes, tries not to think about the non-sense Cal must be filling her head with, tries instead to imagine driving up the lane to the farmhouse tomorrow morning, finding Holly there playing fetch with the dog. He has no idea what he'd say. *Hey, honey bun, remember me?*

Of course it wouldn't be easy. Of course it would take a while to get reacquainted. And so, even as Cal is hanging up, Wylie is thinking, *Okay, fine,* it'd be better to wait until summer anyway, when school is out. They could take a trip together, maybe spend a week or two on the Outer Banks. They could stop at South of the Border. He'd buy her some sparklers, a sombrero, a bag of boiled peanuts for the ride. By then, at least he'd have an apartment.

Wylie's still holding the phone when the recording comes on, telling him to deposit money if he wants to make a call. He puts the receiver in its cradle. Behind the bar, he leaves a five on the counter and digs a Schlitz from the cooler. He doesn't think about it, except to think that the bottle feels good, the weight of it in his hand, flecks of ice sliding off the label. After he gets the first one down, he polishes off two more as fast as his throat will let him, then pauses to wring out the rag and add some more ice. Only then, with the empties lined up on the bar, does it start to sink in: ninety-two days down the tubes. All that thirstiness. All that work.

But he reaches for another anyway, twists off the cap and sends it sailing like a Frisbee over the pool tables. He's not going to beat himself up for *this*. You take a few steps forward, you take a step back. So it goes. The important thing is where you end up. And right now, this is what he needs, whether it takes four beers or forty—a break, a world made smeary enough that he doesn't have to think about tomorrow. Plus, the tremor in his hands is gone. He's steady as a gambler. He puts the rag back where he found it and walks through the bait shop, feels the wind fighting the door as he shoulders his way out onto the pier. Farther down, people are gathered near a grill, the smoke peeling off low and fast. A man with a handlebar mustache is basting shrimp, and Wylie recognizes him as the manager of the pavilion, a guy Hugh once introduced him to, the useful kind of friend Hugh makes when he sits long enough on a bar stool.

At six-foot-seven, Hugh is easy to spot—only today, instead of seersucker and bow tie, he's in swim trunks and flip-flops, showing off a farmer's tan that would keep most men in a shirt. When he sees Wylie coming down the pier, he breaks into a lopsided grin and wades through the crowd, waving a lobster arm above his fish-white belly.

"Damn, Wylie," he says. "You beat up somebody's fist with your face?" He gooses Wylie in the ribs—the same knucklehead greeting Wylie got back in June when they ran into each other at the courthouse, right after he'd finished meeting with his probation officer. Even though they hadn't seen each other since college, Hugh didn't hesitate. "Come work for me," he'd said. "Easy money. Tide you over until you find something that suits."

It isn't until Hugh clinks his bottle against Wylie's that he realizes something isn't right. His gaze travels from Wylie's black eye to the bottle in Wylie's hand, then back again, as if he's connecting the dots in a puzzle. "You get beat up *and* fall off the wagon?"

Wylie's in no mood. His hands may be steady, but his eye feels like it's big as a golf ball. He pulls the return-of-service from his pocket. "That's it. I'm done."

"Done?" Hugh says. "Now wait a skinny minute—" but one look at Wylie and he takes the sheet of paper, folds it into his waistband with a sympathetic nod. "She give you trouble?"

"No more than usual." Wylie hadn't bothered picking up the rest of the papers in the parking lot. Now he doesn't bother telling Hugh that Tracy has taken Ted. He's the lawyer, let him figure it out.

"Listen," Hugh says. "Forget about it. I got some girls I want you to meet, couple of foxes."

"Not today."

"Come on, Sport Model. It's a party."

Wylie swallows what's left in his bottle, rifles a nearby cooler, and comes up empty. "No more beer?"

"There's more down yonder," Hugh says, but he's already talking to Wylie's back. "Catch me before you leave. I've got your check in the car."

"Keep it."

Near the end of the pier, a group of people are shouting and leaning over the rail. At first Wylie thinks someone has fallen in. Then, as he gets closer, he sees a rope ladder, a stringy young guy in cutoffs climbing up from the water. It takes him a moment to understand that the kid has been down there getting battered by the waves, a kind of daredevil game—like riding a mechanical bull, minus the off-switch. When the kid hauls himself back up onto the pier, dripping and sucking wind, the crowd gives him a round of applause.

"Man oh man," somebody says. "You look like a cat in a car wash, Roy."

Still gasping for air, Roy rakes his wet hair off his face and tells the guy to kiss his ass.

"Pick a spot," his friend says. "You're *all* ass."

And everybody is laughing until Roy reaches for a towel and they see the long red scrapes down his side where he's been pitched against the piling. Roy's friend lets out a low whistle, says they better call it a day before somebody gets killed, but Roy is already lighting up a smoke, insisting on another volunteer. Step right up, he's hollering. Who's got what it takes?

It's a carnival barker's call, the kind of taunt Wylie might hear next summer if he were to find himself at Family Kingdom with Holly, strolling past the ring toss or the shooting gallery, and he pictures himself aiming at ducks like any good father would do for his girl, like he'll ever get that chance. Roy is still running his mouth as Wylie balls up his shirt and kicks off his loafers. By the time he's on the ladder, they've formed a circle at the rail. The laughter has died down again. Maybe it's the black eye.

"I'd take off that watch if I was you," Roy says. "And make sure you loop your arms through the rungs."

Down below, a medium-sized wave slaps the bottom of the ladder. Wylie starts to lower himself, pauses after a few rungs, and surveys the distant beach. Deserted. Even the surfers have called it a day. Just a long row of stilted houses that might not be around tomorrow.

He imagines himself, come sunrise, walking through the wreckage with Holly. Only so many chances to see up close what a hurricane can do, and it seems to him there's something he could teach her there, though what, he's not sure. Lessons about calamity, maybe, and picking up the pieces. When his feet reach the bottom rung, the first few waves aren't much, just enough to catch him at the waist and send him slowly swinging between the pilings. It's as if the sea is taking a breather. But Wylie doesn't have to wait long before he sees a big one rising up like *Jaws* behind two or three smaller waves. Judging from the noise on the pier, they see it, too.

"Oh, mama!" Roy shouts. "That one there's supposed to be *mine*."

Of course the waves look bigger down here, face to face, but even so, Wylie has never seen anything like this—a vertical plane of water that almost brushes the underside of the pier as it swells forward, big enough to pluck a man from the ladder as easy as a farmer picking a peach. To Wylie, it seems like the whole day has funneled down into this one moment, and as he gets ready, as the wave suddenly blocks out the sky and the wind, what he's thinking is, *Bring it on.*

Maybe it's the angle of his swing. Maybe the wave isn't ready to break. Or maybe it's because he spins around and it catches him from behind. But before Wylie knows it, he has slid up the wave's face like a buoy, passing through the crest with barely a splash—almost as if it had been a wall of fog and not water, almost as if he wasn't even there.

174

CHAPTER EIGHT

2007

Holly

I'd long since given up on my father, but Lyle couldn't leave well enough alone. He finally turned up his name on the website of some racetrack called the Indianapolis Speedrome, which billed itself as "Home of the World Figure 8." There was a photo, too, a martini toothpick of a man ID'd as Wylie Greer, winner of the July 12 feature race, Bomber division. Checkered flag in hand, he stood leaning against a banged-up Caprice in front of a sign that read VICTORY LANE. He wore a pained smile, as if a bird had just shit on his head: yes, it's supposed to be good luck, but it sure doesn't feel that way.

Lyle tapped the screen. "That's him, right?"

"So what if it is?" But I glanced long enough to know.

That night, I took out a sheet of engraved stationery and wrote him in care of the track.

Dear Father,

  First of all, I'd like thank you for the gracious (if irregular) financial support you provided me in the years following my mother's death. I understand that you and my grandfather had no formal arrangement and that you were under no legal obligation to continue sending money. It has

*always been my assumption that you were acting in good
faith, providing for me as best your circumstances permitted.
Of course, I also assume you realize your contributions
were inadequate.*

*Here's your opportunity to rectify the situation. I'm
writing to request $28,800 in back payment of child support
for the twelve years between my sixth and eighteenth birth-
days (12 years = 144 months × $200). I admit this is an
arbitrary figure, no doubt well below what a judge would
have ordered, never mind interest or inflation. Please contact
me at your earliest convenience to work out a mutually
agreeable payment schedule, and thanks in advance for your
continued commitment to meeting your paternal obligations.*

Your daughter,
Holly Greer

*P.S.—All monies received will be placed in a college
savings fund for my daughter, Claire, and you will be provided copies of the deposit receipts. (Congratulations. You
have a granddaughter. She's ten.)*

Knowing my father's whereabouts unsettled me more than
I cared to admit. At the antique mall that week, while Lyle
was up front with customers and I was in the office dealing
with the online auctions, I found myself at the website again
and again, studying my father's photo and wondering if
he'd ever visited our site to do the same. Wondering why he
was so thin. Wondering if he was ill. I was still trying to break
this habit when, six days after I mailed the letter, a FedEx
envelope arrived from Indianapolis.

I slipped out to the loading dock and drew a cigarette

from the pack Lyle kept stashed there. It had been almost thirty years since I'd heard from my father. He'd stopped calling when I was seven, though I'd received cash in dribs and drabs until I turned eighteen, loose bills that arrived in envelopes with no return address—unlike this one.

I hadn't wanted his money then, and I didn't want it now. I'd only been trying to rankle him. It took two smokes before I worked up the nerve to open the envelope. Inside were ten hundred-dollar bills and a brief note written in palsied, back-slanting script.

> *Dear Holly,*
>   *The day your letter arrived was one of the happiest of my life. Last summer, when you didn't return my calls or reply to my postcards, I could only assume you were through with me. Then, out of the blue, your letter. When can I see you? When can I meet Claire? It would mean the world to me. I'll meet you anytime, anywhere, and of course you are always welcome in my home.*
>   *With hopes of seeing you soon,*
>   *Wylie*

No doubt I'd have been deeply touched by my father's words had they not been a big, steaming pile of b.s. I flicked my cigarette into the weeds and marched back inside. Lyle was at the register, pricing a collection of old fishing lures. I thrust the letter at him and waited for him to finish it.

"I mean, really," I said. "Can you believe?"

Lyle just shook his head. "I suppose it's possible he dialed the wrong number, or got the address wrong."

"I suppose it's possible he's just a pathological liar."

It was bad enough he'd strung me along as a child. Now,

after all these years, for him to say he wanted to see me, to go so far as claiming he'd actually tried to reach me—it was more than I could stand. That night, against my better judgment, I told Claire to pack a suitcase, we were going to Indianapolis.

Lyle frowned. "Don't take the bait."

"It's not bait," I said. "It's a bluff. And I'm calling it."

I remember the car rides best, weekend trips to the tracks at Martinsville, Rockingham, Darlington. I remember the drivers' names, too: Buddy Baker, David Pearson, Cale Yarborough. Once upon a time, that was the company my mother wanted to keep, when she and my father dreamed of winning the Southern 500. By the time I came along, though, they'd sold their '62 Fairlane and settled for being fans. We'd leave before dawn on Saturday morning, arrive at the track in time for qualifying, pitch a tent in the infield overnight, then watch the Grand National race on Sunday afternoon. We traveled in my father's pride and joy, a chocolate-brown, turbocharged 1973 Pontiac Firebird Formula 455, one of only five hundred or so made, but unlike most Formulas, ours didn't have the big firebird decal on the hood because that's where my mother had drawn the line. On the way to and from the races, I'd lean between the bucket seats and sing along to my father's Jim Reeves tapes. Sometimes we played a game where you got points for spotting certain things: a dualie, a speed trap, a box turtle crossing the highway. Other times my father would offer me a penny for every new word I read on the billboards we passed, and I'd try to earn enough for a Reese's by the time we stopped for gas and more beer.

I also had a job, which was manning the ice chest. The

big red Hamilton Kotch Cold Flyte took up half the back-seat. When my father cocked an empty over his shoulder, I'd glance around for smokeys, whip the can out the window, then fish out a cold one. At which point my father would wink at me in the rearview and crack wise. "Thank you, Nurse." "Is there an angel in the car?" I assumed this was how all families passed the time on car rides.

The trip was a smooth one until we hit stop-and-go traffic on I-640. Claire put down her *Sports Illustrated for Kids* and stared up at a truck-stop sign advertising diesel and free showers. She'd long since outgrown the billboard game, though not before amassing a small fortune in copper she donated to the local cat shelter. "Do you think I'll be taller than five-seven?" she said, stretching out her legs. "That's how tall Jeff is." Jeff was NASCAR champion Jeff Gordon, her current heartthrob and the square-jawed subject of a poster tacked above her bed. She'd been sharing bits of Jeff lore with me throughout the trip, occasioned by the fact that Pittsboro, near Indianapolis, was his adopted hometown.

I'd yet to mention that her grandfather raced cars. In fact, I'd yet to mention he was alive. The story had always been that both of my parents died as a result of the boating acci-dent. Not telling Claire the truth had been easier than trying to explain how a father could just up and leave his daughter. Since Wylie's letter, I'd been trying to craft an explanation that took into account his side of things but at the same time not letting him off the hook, but I wasn't having much luck, and so, as we merged onto I-75, I simply laid out the facts. This wasn't actually an antiques-hunting trip, I told her. Not strictly speaking. The main reason we were going to

Indianapolis was to visit my father, who as it happened wasn't really dead. I told her the story of how, on the day of my mother's funeral, he'd dropped me off at Cal's farm. He said he'd be back soon, and that was that.

Claire lowered her magazine and studied her knees. "Um, I'd like to buy a vowel, please?"

"I know. It's pretty crazy. I'm sorry I didn't tell you sooner. I didn't know where to start."

Claire nodded. Suddenly I felt overwhelmed. I wished Lyle were there to take the wheel, but he'd stayed home to look after the mall, which he'd been doing a lot of since his dad retired and they sold the company. The truth was, I'd been looking forward to having Claire all to myself. Now I fiddled with the radio, checked the odometer, adjusted my seat. After a few miles, Claire reached over without looking up and patted my knee. The knot in my stomach loosened. If any ten-year-old could handle this, she could. She was a star at Heathwood Hall. As the counselor, Mr. Lindy, once put it, "You have your garden-variety gifted kids, and then you have kids like Claire." Now she was examining the contents of the brown-bag lunch Lyle had packed for us: turkey and Swiss on rye, low-fat trail mix, Bartlett pears.

"So is he supposed to be like my grandfather now?"

"He *is* your grandfather."

She sighed. "You know what I mean."

I told her I wouldn't get my hopes up. She opened one of the Ziplocs, pillaged the Swiss, then dropped the rest of the sandwich back into the bag.

The track sat alongside a rail bed in an industrial area on the city's fringe. It reminded me of the dirt bullring they once had in Columbia, only the Drome, as it seemed to be known, was paved, with no infield. Claire and I stood in the summer dusk at a chain-link fence that separated the stands from the track. At lunch, she'd been excited to hear about the evening's entertainment. She informed me, between bites of her Big Mac, that Jeff Gordon sometimes raced incognito at small tracks as a way of staying close to his roots. Now she seemed doubtful that he'd be caught dead in such a place. "Hey," she said, "why don't we put some bleachers around this parking lot and call it a racetrack?"

We bought general admission seats and made our way into the stands. It was a beer-and-corn-dogs crowd, little kids covered in ketchup, shirtless young guys with tattoos, mothers balancing infants on their knees as they lit cigarettes. While I looked for the earplugs Lyle had sent along, Claire studied the program and gave me the lowdown. We were just in time for the Bomber Figure 8s, which was the main event on Friday nights. A beginner's division, she said, excitedly pointing to a list of drivers that included my father. I resisted her enthusiasm, letting my eyes fall instead on an ad for the "Rent a Hornet" program. *Are you not sure that racing is for you? Try our Rent a Hornet program.* For $75, you got a car, practice laps, heat, feature, and a trophy.

The crowd perked up as the Bombers began filing through a corrugated metal gate on the far side of the track. Everybody in the stands seemed to know one or another of the drivers, calling out to them as they lined up. Most of the cars looked as if they'd been decorated with a bucket of paint and a stick. Here and there a copilot was visible: stuffed Pooh bears and Elmos lashed to the passenger seats. My father was the last car onto the track. He had his arm out the window, fingers drumming the door above a silver eleven, my mother's old number. As he took his place among the other cars, my throat went dry. I could just make out his face, the slight upturn of his nose that made him look younger than he was. Claire stood and cheered as they announced his name over the loudspeaker. When I shot her a look, she shot it right back.

"Like you said, he *is* my grandfather."

On the day my father dropped me off at Cal's farm, I remember standing out front, waving good-bye and trying to be brave—after all, he said he'd be gone only a few days—but as he eased down the lane, careful not to kick up dust, I could feel myself starting to lose it. Cal was standing behind me with his hands planted on my shoulders. I ducked away and broke into a run, the grass and trees blurring green all around me. I'd almost caught up to the Firebird when my father stuck his arm out the window to wave, only it wasn't his arm, it was his leg, bare toes wiggling a dainty adios. Cornball stunts were a specialty of his. He'd always been able to make me smile, even in the dark days between my mother's death and her funeral. I came to a stop by the mailbox at the end of the lane. My father never slowed down, but he never pulled his foot in, either. It was still poking out the window as he turned onto Bluff Road and sped off into the afternoon.

Once the Bomber race started, I understood why the Drome had no infield. Instead of circling the oval's perimeter, the cars traveled in a figure eight. By the fourth lap, they were crossing paths in the middle of the track. How the drivers avoided colliding, I don't know. Some barreled into the crossfire at top speed while others were more timid, stutter-braking their way through the oncoming traffic. My father was the most timid of all. He started the race in last place and finished in last place, completing only eighteen of twenty laps. Not that Claire minded; she never stopped cheering. She even jumped up onto her seat the one time Wylie passed another car, which he managed to do only because the other driver spun out. But I was too distracted to ask her to sit down. Despite the fact that my father's driving was cautious as a nun's, my palms had begun to sweat against the aluminum seat. It annoyed me that I cared, but I hadn't come all that way just to see him get killed.

After the race, we headed for the pit area along a pocked concourse that ran behind the bleachers. The smell of gasoline hung in the air. Above us, clouds parted to reveal a silvery slice of moon.

"Why'd he leave?" Claire said, pocketing her earplugs.

I stared up at the sky, thinking about all the time I'd wasted wondering the same thing. "I don't know," I said. "He never told me." And I didn't plan on asking. After all these years, I wasn't going to give him the chance to make excuses.

"Maybe he didn't think he could raise you all by himself."

"Or maybe he thought Cal would do a better job," I said. "Maybe I reminded him of my mother. Maybe he was punishing himself. Or maybe he never wanted kids in the first place. It doesn't really matter, does it?"

Claire took my hand as we approached the fence that encircled the pit area. A rent-a-cop sat on a stool by the gate, but he didn't bat an eye as we strolled past. Inside, the place looked like a cross between a junkyard and a swap

WILL ALLISON

meet. Drivers were busy hitching up cars, loading up tool-boxes, sweet-talking their girlfriends. My father had just finished winching his Bomber to the back of his pickup. He spotted us coming through the crowd. For a moment he stood stock-still, a grin slowly creasing his face, then he turned to open the door of his truck. I thought he was making a run for it, just like he'd done the last time I came looking for him, but he was only retrieving something from the glove box—a video camera. He filmed us right up until we reached the truck, then set the camcorder on the hood and opened his wiry arms to gather us in for a hug.

Of all the footage from that weekend, that's the part I've watched the most: the big reunion scene. I'd often thought that when I finally found him, the first thing I'd do was haul off and give him a knuckle sandwich—his phrase—but as I closed the distance between us, I opted instead for a look of stony indifference, one that would make clear I wasn't buying whatever it was he was selling. The tape tells a different story, though. On the screen, dragging Claire behind me, I angle straight into his arms like a homing pigeon, hard-wired instinct overriding all else. He's thin, yes—I can feel ribs through the back of his shirt—but there's nothing frail about him. And then, as he's holding us tight and I'm left gazing over his shoulder at the camera, the look on my face is positively desperate. Suddenly I'm five years old again, clinging to his neck as he trundles me away from the hole in the ground where they've just put my mother.

•   •   •

186

At first, of course, I assumed he was drunk, just as I assumed he'd been drunk since the day he disappeared. How else to account for his confusion, his utter bewilderment during those first awkward moments we spent standing around, trying to figure out what to say to one another? I started by introducing Claire, who immediately asked for a ride in his Bomber. He said no, the car wasn't street legal, but she was welcome to sit in it. In the course of five minutes, he proceeded to ask her three times how old she was, and then he asked if he'd already asked. But even as he bumbled along, there was a sliver of self-awareness about him—a twinkle in his eye that said, *I'm not quite right, but don't worry, folks, it's okay, because I know I'm not quite right.* Maybe that's why, instead of being freaked out, Claire took a shine to him. The third time he asked how old she was, she rested a forearm on the steering wheel and squinted up at him. "I'm ten," she said. "Same as the last time you asked."

"Maybe so," my father said, "but you'll be eleven before I remember it."

The details of my father's medical condition came out later, back at his place. He was living in a cedar-shingle bungalow in a quiet neighborhood not far from the Drome. For supper, he fixed us pancakes. Claire asked how come we never had pancakes for supper. "Because pancakes are for breakfast," I said. We were sitting at the kitchen table, watching my father pour batter into a skillet. His hands shook. Occasionally he paused to consult a memo pad he kept in his shirt pocket, one time adding a note with a small, blunt pencil, just like the ones he and I used to pilfer from Putt Putt. The camcorder, now mounted on a tripod, recorded our every move, and each time Claire noticed it, she fell into a conniption of fake preening.

"Mind if we shut that thing off?" I said.

My father pulled a plate of bacon from the microwave. "Ever hear of Korsakoff's syndrome?"

I shook my head.

"How do you spell it?" Claire said.

He spelled it for her as he served us stacks of buckwheat pancakes. For himself, he'd prepared a bowl of rabbit food—a salad of kale and radishes and baby spinach dressed only with vinegar. Once he'd arranged his napkin in his lap, he tapped the side of his head like he was testing a cantaloupe and told us it all started with his old buddy Jim Beam. "What I'm saying is, I had a drinking problem." A serious one. Near the end, he'd pretty much stopped eating. The result was a severe thiamine deficiency, which was what triggered the seizure. This was last summer, a Friday night. Luckily, a neighbor called 911 after stumbling, literally, upon my father, who was lying on the sidewalk still clutching a bottle in his fist. At least this was what they told my father. He woke in the hospital with no recollection of the seizure, his wallet missing, his short-term memory shot to hell. "It's screwy," he said. "I can still remember the name of every kid in my kindergarten class, but half the time I can't remember what happened five minutes ago. And it was worse—a *lot* worse—right after the seizure. Now it's not so bad, unless I forget my pills. Unless I get flustered."

Claire nodded along solemnly as I surveyed the color-coded Post-Its that covered the fridge, the bottles of medication on the counter. I hadn't seen so many pills since my grandfather's last days. This was, as Cal would've said, like déjà vu all over again—the difference being my father seemed determined to live.

"So I get it," I said. "The camcorder's for when you forget we were even here."

This came out sounding meaner than I intended, but my father didn't seem to mind. "Repetition helps," he said. "If I watch the tape enough times, it'll take. And this"—he spread his hands, like a statue of a saint—"is something I don't want to forget."

On the TV screen, my father and I sit side by side in wicker chairs on his front porch, awash in grainy, yellowish light. He hasn't touched a drop of alcohol since the seizure. Even the fake beer we're drinking is officially off limits, on account of his diet. Tonight's a special occasion, though. "You got to kick up your heels sometime," he says, clinking his bottle against mine.

Actually, I could use a real drink. I've just put Claire to bed and joined him on the porch, intending to discuss his letter. For once, I'm glad the camcorder's there. I want this on the record. But before I can raise the subject, my father's off on a long dissertation about his diet. He credits his miraculous, albeit partial, recovery to something called calorie restriction, which he's quick to point out isn't about weight loss but about fighting disease and slowing the aging process. He says there's proof that calorie restriction leads to longer, healthier lives in lab animals, the theory being that it somehow forces the body to tap into dormant, little-understood powers of self-healing. "Some of these rats are living *forty percent* longer," he says. "Think about it. That's like a person living to be a hundred and twenty."

I'm not convinced living that long is such a good idea, but I have bigger fish to fry than debating the merits of starving yourself. I drain the last of my beer and stare for a moment at the camera. "You didn't really try to get in touch with me," I say.

"Pardon?" He's in the middle of a detailed description of his meals—something about "alternate-day fasting"—but he stops short as I pull the letter from my pocket and hand it to him. He holds the page up to the light. I lean over and point to the offending line.

"That's not true," I say. "The last time you called me was July eleventh, 1978. Cal answered the phone."

My father squints as if he's having trouble keeping me in focus. In fact, the camcorder has autofocused on the window behind us, so we're both a bit blurry.

"But I did," he said. "Right after I got out of the hospital."

"I was listening at the top of the stairs. Cal told you to stop calling and getting my hopes up. By the time I got to the other phone, you'd already hung up."

"I left five or six messages on your machine," he said. "I tried you at work. I even sent a certified letter, but nobody signed for it."

"Nobody signed for it because it never came, and it never came because you never sent it." I'm rising from my chair now, wagging a finger at him and looking slightly crazed. It's not my finest moment. "I can't believe I'm even having this conversation."

My father slumps into his chair and makes a soft hissing sound, like a radiator giving up the ghost.

A couple weeks before Cal told him to stop calling, I spoke with my father for the last time. He was renting a room in Beaufort, working at a Texaco. By then he'd been gone almost two years, time I'd spent wondering what I'd done to make him leave and what I could do to make him come back. When pleading didn't work, I tried lies. I'd been diagnosed with leukemia (a classmate's misfortune), I was running off to South America to join a commune (something I'd seen on TV), Cal beat me with a rake (he'd only joked about doing so).

But on this day—the day of our last conversation—I tried a different tack. In my time with Cal, I'd come to understand it wasn't so easy for a man to raise a little girl all by himself. So I tried bargaining with my father. If he let me come live with him, I said, I'd cook his meals, clean his room, iron his shirts. I'd get a job after school to help with the bills. I'd keep him company now that Mom was gone.

Usually, no matter what I said, he'd just tell me to hang in there, he'd be back soon. Not this time, though. "Goddammit," he said, cutting me off. "Stop it, honey bun. Just stop." It was the first time I could remember him talking to me like that. I held my breath, afraid to breathe, afraid he'd hang up if I said another word. Outside, Cal was cutting the grass, turning circles around the weeping willow atop his little John Deere. Our coon dog, Leo, followed close behind, barking at the mower. Finally my father spoke. "Look," he said. He wasn't angry anymore. "You're not the reason I left, okay? Do you understand, Holly? None of this is your fault. No matter what happens, I want you to remember that." I was still too scared to speak. Something about his voice wasn't right, the way it rose and wavered. By the time he got to "I love you," it sounded as though the words were made of water.

* * *

Before I went to bed, I called Lyle and filled him in on my father, his illness, his plans to live forever, his stubborn insistence that he'd tried to get in touch with me. I told him I was ready to come home. Lyle offered to catch a plane to Indianapolis.

"No," I said. "I'll be fine. It's just one more night."

"Of all the things to lie about," Lyle said. "I still don't get it."

"He just wants to pretend he finally got off his ass and did what he should have done years ago. He wants credit he doesn't deserve."

Lyle said, "How's Claire holding up?"

When I woke at six, Claire wasn't in bed. I found her at the kitchen table with my father, who'd just finished giving her his spiel on calorie restriction. It's not easy, he was saying, but when the hunger started getting to him, all he had to do was think of me and Claire, the extra years he'd have with us. As I walked in, he cleared his throat, studied his corned beef hash.

"Grandpa has a surprise for us," Claire said, slathering butter on toast. "But we have to get there early."

"'Grandpa'?"

My father held a chair for me. A cup of coffee sat waiting. "Claire informs me I failed to mention the surprise last night. I probably thought I had and didn't want to repeat myself. That's the problem with poor short-term memory. You either say something ten times or you forget to say it at all."

I stared at the fried eggs atop his hash. I wasn't going to let him get to me again. He knew I didn't believe him; that

192

was enough. I put on a bright smile. "What happened to Grandpa's wonder diet?"

He reflected the smile right back at me, but it was Claire who answered. "It's a nonfasting day," she said. "He gets to eat like a hog."

My father's dream was to be a mechanic for a big-time NASCAR outfit, and in the early 1980s, he headed for North Carolina, center of the NASCAR universe. While he waited for an opportunity to present itself, he put in time at various garages in and around Charlotte, but it's hard to hold down a job when you're too hung over to come to work, and eventually he found himself repairing minibikes and go-karts instead of real cars. He was good with the little engines, though, and his boss liked him, and soon he wasn't just repairing karts, he was building them. Their scale and simplicity spoke to him. The miniature engines were a perfect puzzle. When he got the chance, through a friend of a friend, to move into custom racing karts at a dealership in Indianapolis, he didn't hesitate. That was eight years ago.

"These babies here," he said, escorting us through the showroom, "they go for about ten grand." The room smelled of new tires. My father beamed as Claire moved from kart to kart, testing them out. He patted one of the seats. "Hand-laid Italian fiberglass," he said. Claire announced that Jeff Gordon had gotten his start racing karts. "At age *five*," she said with reverence. Next on the tour was the service area, where karts sat in varying states of repair. Our shoes squeaked on the glossy floor. My father's workbench looked just like his kitchen counter, plastered with Post-Its and checklists. "They just think I'm organized," he said, unlocking the back door.

Outside, an elaborate asphalt track filled the lot behind the building. There were bleachers, an electric starting pole, even a small replica of the Indianapolis Motor Speedway's famed pagoda. My father smiled and pointed the camcorder at us. This was the surprise.

"Shop doesn't open till nine," he said, "so that gives us two hours."

We had the track all to ourselves. Right off Claire asked if she could ride alone, which was fine with my father—apparently, lots of kids race karts, not just future NASCAR champs—but I told her she'd have to start out riding with me. While she sulked, my father outfitted us with helmets, gave us a brief tutorial, then suggested I tail him around the track until I got the hang of it. With Claire wedged safely between my legs, I fired up the kart and followed him out of the paddock.

At first it was hard to keep up, even though he was going slow. The pedals were more responsive than I expected, and as I struggled to find a rhythm between the brakes and gas, Claire feigned whiplash, letting her head flop like a rag doll's. By the end of the second lap, though, I was getting a feel for the kart, champing at the bit to go faster. I opened up the throttle. For the next ten minutes or so, we circled the track at a good clip. Naturally, I set my sights on catching my father, though I tried not to be too obvious about it; after all, we were there for Claire. Not that I had a prayer of catching him anyway. He knew the track too well, he wasn't carrying extra weight, and he probably had more horsepower. Every time I was on the verge of overtaking him, he'd accelerate just a little. If I didn't know better, I'd have said he was taunting me. Finally, after he'd twirled a finger in the air to signal his last lap, I made my move. We were coming into a sweeping turn. I cut wide, gunned the engine, and nearly put the kart into the guardrail before I wrangled it back under control. Claire stiffened, holding on for dear life. "Jesus, Mom!"

A minute later, hands still trembling, I pulled alongside my father and shut off the engine. Despite the close call, I wasn't ready to quit. I wanted another crack at him, just the two of us out there. It was time for his medicine, though, which he said made him too dizzy to drive, and besides, he wanted some footage of me and Claire.

"In one kart or two?" she said.

At that point, I felt like I owed her. "All yours," I said, climbing out. "But if I see you hotdogging it, I'm waving you in."

"Hello, Pot," she said. "I'm Kettle."

I ignored her and turned back to my father, who was replacing the camcorder's battery. I'd decided that what we needed was a level playing field.

"You ever rent a Hornet?" I said.

Once, not long before the skiing accident, my parents took me for a spin on a real racetrack. This was out in Cayce, at the old Columbia Speedway. After the races, if you were so inclined, they'd let you take a couple laps in your car. We waited in line behind the other wannabes and then, when the flagger gave us the go-ahead, my father popped the Firebird's clutch and off we went. The track was bumpier than I expected, and narrower. By the time we hit the backstretch, it felt like we were doing 150, but the speedometer was pegged at 60. I was up front, sitting on my mother's lap. After the first time around, I remember my father asking if she wanted to drive, which made a lot of sense, given her experience and relative sobriety. "No, thanks," she said. "I'm retired, remember?" My father wouldn't let it go. "Come on," he said. "One lap. For old times' sake." Later, on the drive home, my mother was quiet. She didn't want to talk about the race. She didn't want to sing. She just smoked and stared out the window. And though I knew she'd chosen to become a mother—though I knew she'd given up racing for that very reason—I couldn't shake the feeling that she thought she'd made a mistake.

On the videotape, you can hear us, but you don't see us. All you see is Claire making her way through the turns at a sensible speed, waving like a beauty queen each time she passes us. I'm in the bleachers with my father, trying to convince him to rent a Hornet. It's not just that I want to race him, and beat him; there's more to it than that. A long time ago, I came to the conclusion that the only way my father could have done what he did—the only way he could live with himself—was to put me out of his mind, will himself to forget. And what I wanted now was not so much an apology or an explanation as for him simply to remember, to *register* what had been lost. To feel a hunger in his heart like the one I'd been carrying around. And what better way than to make him see my mother in me? What better place than a racetrack?

My father's having none of it, though. "There's a reason they make you sign your life away before you get in one of those sardine cans," he says.

"Like figure eight's any safer?"

"Why would I rent a race car when I already own one?"

"Come on," I say. "My treat. Mom would be proud." He

turns to me then, forgetting the camcorder, and my face fills
the screen, hair boxy from the helmet. For the first time, I
notice he still wears his wedding band, and I'd like to believe
he's thinking about the happy life we once had, how brokenhearted my mother would be to know how it all turned
out. "Your mother—" he says, but before he can finish,
Claire's engine cuts out. The camera pans back to the track,
where she's parking the kart. As she strolls over, I call out to
her, ask how she'd like to man the camera while Grandpa and
I take on all comers in the Hornet division. Right away, she
loves the idea. "It'll be like Dale and Dale Junior," she says.

My father's on the spot. He doesn't want to let her
down. Even so, he complains about the nature of oval racing
versus figure eight. "Just going around in circles," he says.
"It's metaphorically disturbing."

Helmet tucked under her arm, Claire gives this a little
thought. "But isn't a figure eight just a circle with a twist?"

My father was the one driving the boat when my mother hit
the dock. We talked about this only once, on the way to
Cal's after the funeral. My father asked if I thought he was to
blame and I told him no.

"Your grandfather does," he said.

"It was an accident."

"There was a sailboat," he said. "I had to hug the shore."

And then I said what we both knew to be true. "She was
showing off."

I didn't see the accident, but I heard it. That summer, my
mother had been toying with the idea of competitive skiing.
While she and my father practiced slalom runs, I lay on the
other side of the cove, sunning myself on the little patch of

sand that passed for a beach at our lake cabin. It was the fifth of July, and I'd just finished collecting empty beer cans and spent roman candles left over from our annual bash, filling a plastic lawn bag that rattled like Mardi Gras. Now I watched my mother carve arcs of water in the glassy lake, sometimes veering toward a dock and cutting away at the last second, her elbow almost grazing the surface as she hung a curtain of water above the sun-bleached boards. After a while, drowsy from the sun, I closed my eyes. I was almost asleep when I heard it: a dull, wooden thud followed by a sudden drop in the outboard's idle, two heartbeats of nothing, then the full-throttle sound of my father churning white water, racing back to her. As soon as he'd hauled her on board, he fired a flare, and for a moment, before I understood I was to run inside and call for help, I just sat there on the beach staring at the burst of red. Compared to the previous night's fireworks, it barely scratched the sky.

Back at the house, after I'd called the Drome and given them my credit card information, I asked my father if he had any pictures of my mother. He hauled out an old suitcase I recognized from childhood, the red American Tourister that used to accompany us on our weekend trips to the races. Inside were two photo albums and a pair of gray coveralls my mother had worn as a racing uniform. Claire's interest was piqued.

"Was she any good?"

"Was she any *good*?" My father rolled his eyes. "Jeff Gordon couldn't carry your grandmother's jockstrap."

One of the albums held family photos—including pictures of me—but my father started with the other one, which was devoted to my mother's racing career. With the camcorder rolling, the three of us sat on the living room rug as he told us about each picture. His anecdotes confirmed what he'd said about Korsakoff's: his long-term memory was intact, sharp as a pocketknife. What surprised me, though, was how few of the stories I'd heard before, stories I had a right to know but didn't. For instance, my mother had been involved in at least four on-the-track crashes. ("The other drivers had it in for her," he said. "They thought she should stick to the powder puff races.") One photo showed her being pulled by two medics from an overturned car. In another, she's pointing to the car's smashed fender, her arm in a plaster cast.

Not only did the photos leave me feeling cheated, they were also starting to make me nervous about the Hornet race. I went into the kitchen for a glass of water. While I was at the sink, I overheard my father explaining to Claire why, after a lifetime on the sidelines, *he'd* taken up racing as well. Claire had commandeered the camcorder and was training it on him like a seasoned documentary filmmaker. "First time I saw a figure-eight race," he was saying, "I knew Maddy would have loved it. But we didn't have figure eight back then. Not around Columbia. So I sort of tried it on her behalf." The reason he kept at it—"and, obviously, it's not because I'm any good"—was that he'd yet to find anything else that made him feel closer to her. Which was funny, he said, because he'd spent so many years trying to get *away* from her (Jim Beam presumably being his key accomplice). It wasn't until he moved to Indiana, far from any patch of earth he and my mother ever shared, that he realized he probably ought to be holding on to her memory, not running from it. "When I'm out on the track," he said, "I swear, it's like she's right there in the car with me." Later I'd see that

199

Claire opted for a tight close-up during this moment. As for me, I was still in the kitchen, waiting to see if he'd get to the part about how he had run from me, too, but I suppose that's a story he wasn't ready to tell Claire, or even himself.

The antique stores were just a short walk from my father's house, but first I stopped for a pack of ultra lights and sat on a bench in front of the library, trying to put out of my mind the image of Claire surrounded by those photographs and gazing at my father, rapt as a disciple. I'd left the house in a hurry, telling them I had to get busy if I had any hope of justifying this trip. Now I started with the nearest antique store, moving decisively through the cramped aisles, feeling in full control for the first time since I'd set foot in Indianapolis. On a real buying trip, of course, I'd stick to private collections, estate sales, antique shows—places with stuff worth traveling for. Even so, as I worked my way down a strip of mom-and-pop shops, I managed to pick up a decent Hoosier cabinet and a few advertising pieces for a Bennigan's that Lyle and I were outfitting that summer. The find of the afternoon was a set of six ornate oak doors, original 1890s hardware intact, salvaged from some poor Queen Anne that had been "updated" by its new owner. I made arrangements to pick up everything later, and by the time I was done, I'd bought enough to fill the little U-Haul I planned to get for the ride home.

It was almost four, the late afternoon sun glinting off windshields of passing cars. We were due at the Drome soon to sign waivers and take our practice laps. I was halfway back to my father's house when my cell rang. Lyle sounded triumphant.

"It's called confabulation," he said.

"What is?"

"What's going on in your father's brain."

Lyle had been online doing some research. Confabulation, he said, was a classic symptom of Korsakoff's. The patient invents things to fill in the blanks of his memory. Sometimes the details are so convincing that even the doctors are fooled. And of course the patient can't distinguish between the invented memories and real ones. Lyle asked when exactly my father claimed to have called.

"Last summer," I said, taking a seat on the curb. "When he got out of the hospital."

"Bingo. That's when you're most likely to have big gaps in your memory. Right after a seizure."

"So he *is* full of shit," I said. "He just doesn't know it."

"I suppose that's one way of looking at it."

I shaded my eyes and examined a pothole between my feet. Hidden in shadow, the original brick pavers shone beneath thick layers of asphalt. "But what if he's just *faking* confabulation?"

"For Pete's sake," Lyle said.

Sixteen years before he found my father on the Internet, Lyle had the rare pleasure of meeting him face to face. This was right after Cal died, during what would have been my junior year of college, only I'd dropped out and gone into a full tailspin, drinking like my father's daughter. After years of trying not to give a damn, I'd gotten it into my head that I had to find him, the last of my living kin. With a little homework, I managed to piece together a rough sketch of his life, a pattern of drifting from one town to the next, one job to the next, one bottle to the next. Eventually I tracked him down to a service station in Camden, but when I showed up, the owner claimed he no longer worked there. A few days later, hoping he'd have better luck, Lyle went to Camden alone. He ended up in a diner eating lunch with my father, who told him he wanted to be a part of my life but just wasn't ready. Lyle sized Wylie up then and there and decided I was better off without him, better off not even knowing he'd found him. This, of course, was a big mistake on Lyle's part—thinking he had the right to decide what was best for me. When I figured out what was going on, I told him we were done and made for Camden, flask in hand, attracting the attention of the state police along the way. Lyle was after me, too, afraid I'd kill myself in a wreck, and he arrived at the garage just in time to find me once again not finding my father. The troopers showed up a few minutes later. Mindful of my drunkenness but perhaps more mindful of his own plummeting stock, Lyle let the police think he'd been the driver of the car that had just led them on a wild goose chase. He spent thirty days in the Kershaw County Jail, and just like in a fairy tale, we got hitched the day he got out.

As I approached my father's house, I found myself doing a sort of mental calculus, trying to decide if his believing he'd tried to contact me was in fact as good as his having actually done so. I hadn't made up my mind by the time I walked through the door. My father and Claire were still camped out in the living room, only now she was wearing my mother's old racing uniform.

"Grandpa's going to build me a kart!" she said, pivoting like a runway model to show off the uniform's ancient oil stains.

My father gave me a helpless look. "If it's okay with your mom, that is."

"Please, Mom?"

The name MADDY was stitched above her breast pocket. Shiny red stripes ran down the sleeves, which hung past her hands. I turned to my father. "Can I talk to you a sec?" Claire gave me a disappointed look and sank onto the sofa as my father followed me into the hallway.

"She said she wanted one for her birthday," he said. "I'm sorry. It just popped out of my mouth."

"It's not that." I was remembering all the promises he'd once made to me. *I found us a little place at the beach. I'm looking into schools. Shouldn't be more than a month.* I was remembering how, for a while, I'd believed every word, and I was thinking how much I'd like to get him out on the track and run him into a wall. "It's just that I'd appreciate your not writing any checks you can't cash."

For a moment he stared at me as if I'd stomped his foot and he was trying to decide if it was on purpose. Then he glanced back at Claire, who was leafing through a karting magazine from the pile on the end table. "I'll cash 'em," he said, not even looking at me, "so long as the bank's open."

"Come on guys go go go let's give it a little juice and see what those babies can do." On tape, Claire's voice cheers us on as she records our exploits for posterity. This is the heat. Onscreen, the Hornets appear to be moving in slow motion, the whine of their engines like a tired swarm of bees. Inside the car, though, things are happening fast. Too fast for me to think about ramming my father. Too fast for me to do much of anything except squeeze the steering wheel, grit my teeth, and try not to get run over. Whatever confidence I had in the go-kart that morning has vanished in the confusion of so many cars on such a small track.

Early in the race, Claire tries to get fancy with the camera, zooming in, searching out our faces. The result is jittery and disorienting, almost unwatchable. Finally, mercifully, she settles for a wide-angle shot that takes in most of the track. It's the second or third lap, and by now my father and I are already hugging the wall, ceding the inside lane to real contenders as we grimly duke it out for last place. This is not quite the showing Claire has hoped for. Soon she gives up cheering and switches to the voice of a TV announcer. "Ladies and gentlemen, looks like it's going to be a long, long night." The heat drags on for fifteen laps. A couple of times my father makes like he's going to pass me but never quite builds up enough steam. Who can say if he's really even trying? When I cross the finish line ahead of him, the rest of the cars are already lining up to leave.

If my father saw my mother in me as we circled the track, if he felt the pistons of loss firing away inside the worn cylinders of his heart, he didn't show it afterward. All he did was rest a hand on my shoulder and grin. "Guess now we know racing's not genetic."

"Maybe not," I said. "Or maybe I just got *your* genes."

We'd decided to skip the feature and were standing around waiting for the track steward to relieve us of our rentals so we could get back to Claire, who at that very moment was probably trying to locate us with the zoom. My father glanced toward the grandstand, raised his arm in a wave. He'd agreed to this only because she wanted it, and now he was eager to be done. After the steward took our keys and checked the cars for damage, we made our way back in silence, pausing only for a bottle of water so my father could take his pills. He hadn't had much to say since our chat in the hallway.

As we climbed the concrete steps, Claire stood and held her nose. "What's that smell?"

My father stared at his boots and sniffed. "The smell of de-feet?"

"Oh, well," she said. "Them's the brakes."

Where they'd come up with this routine, I had no idea, but as I stood there watching them, it wasn't hard to imagine a day when my father would give up on me completely and move on, concentrating all his efforts on Claire, the clean slate, the fresh start. "How'd you ever win a race anyway?" I said.

He glanced from me to Claire and shrugged. "Used to be I was better in the *clutch*."

"Must have had more *drive* back then," Claire added.

I'd heard enough. I suggested we celebrate with corn dogs and then stop by the office to pick up our hard-earned trophies. On the way down to the concession stand, my father told Claire about his lone victory. Only six cars had been in the Bomber race that night, and three of them were lost in a pileup. Another threw a scrap-iron fit two laps before the finish. "And the last driver was a rookie," he said, "even more of a feather foot than me."

Claire was holding his hand as she guided him through the crowd. "Here," I said, peeling off a twenty. "I'm getting a beer." That's how low I'd sunk, wanting my father to have to watch me enjoy a drink. The beer stand was next to the concession stand. I got in line and was still waiting to place my order when my father started telling Claire how much he was looking forward to visiting her in Columbia. He asked if anyone was living in the cottage he and my mother had rented from Cal before we moved up to the lake. Then he asked if she'd like a go-kart for her birthday. "I'd love one," she said, shooting me a glance. He offered to build her one. Again. "Course, you'll need somewhere to ride it," he said. "A nice little dirt track. Wouldn't be too hard to make one if we could get our hands on a Bobcat." Claire told him we had a tractor. "And there's plenty of room out behind the silo," she said.

During this conversation, I stared at my father, willing him to look my way, but he was oblivious. Had he simply forgotten what I said? Did he not realize he was making promises again? In the end, it didn't matter. What mattered was that Claire believed him—believed *in* him. I watched them doctoring their corn dogs at the condiment table, chatting away like old friends. Bringing her along had been a bad idea. The funny thing was, my first impulse had been to leave her at home, on the grounds that my father wasn't the kind of person I wanted her around, and also that he didn't deserve to know her. But I'd given in to a different kind of selfishness. I'd imagined the ache my father would feel the first time he laid eyes on her, the reckoning of his loss, the ten years he'd already missed. And how could he look at her without thinking of me, too, a young girl standing by a mailbox, shrinking in his rearview mirror? I'd never even stopped to consider the risk to Claire, the possibility she might fall for him so fast, so hard. Now the two of them were drifting over to the souvenir stand to check out the T-shirts. No doubt my father would buy her whatever her heart desired. I turned around, disgusted, and was surprised to find myself looking into the steely blue eyes of none other than Jeff Gordon, a life-sized cardboard cutout with the Budweiser logo emblazoned on his flame-retardant suit. Though I'd never thought much of Claire's crush on him, I decided right then I'd get us tickets to a NASCAR race the minute we got home.

"Next?" The guy behind the counter was staring at me with an amused smile. *Whenever you're ready, lady. Whenever you make it back to Earth.*

I tapped the can of Budweiser in Jeff's hand. "I'll have what Jeff's having."

The guy raised an eyebrow, more amused. "You mean Dale Junior?"

Up until the business in Camden, I'd carried on with my life more or less expecting to turn around someday, at the grocery store or the post office or on a street corner, and catch a glimpse of my father. Often I had the feeling I was being watched. He was simply waiting for the right moment, perhaps one that offered a shot at redemption—a robbery or house fire he could save me from. These, I knew, were thoughts for a child, and after Camden, I began to let go of them. Now and then, driving home or lying in bed, I'd still talk to him in my mind, not the missing Wylie but the young father he'd once been, the two of us retracing conversations we might or might not have really had. Slowly but surely, I learned to keep him in the past, where he belonged, where he couldn't do any more harm.

That night, as soon as I heard him snoring in the next room, I got out of bed, pulled on jeans, and quietly packed our bags. I was waiting until the last possible minute to wake

WILL ALLISON

Claire. She wouldn't want to leave, would want to know why we were sneaking off in the middle of the night without even saying good-bye, and I didn't know how to explain why I couldn't stay. After I'd carried our bags to the door, I made a final sweep of the house, pausing by the phone. Better to wait and call Lyle later, once we were on the road; in the morning, he could arrange shipment of the stuff I'd bought at the antique shops. Turning to get Claire, I noticed the blinking red light of the camcorder recharging on the mantel and, beside it, the five or six videotapes my father had made since we arrived. It occurred to me that there might come a time when I'd want to hear his stories about my mother—the ones I'd missed while I was out—but I didn't know which tape was which. The labels weren't annotated, just numbered. As I sifted through the pile, I felt a pinprick of guilt. I could picture my father turning the house upside down, wondering if he'd misplaced a tape or simply misnumbered them. And without the tape, would he even remember the time he'd spent looking at those photos with Claire? I decided I didn't care; he'd already gotten more of us than he deserved. In fact, the tapes alone were more than he deserved, the memories they held no more his than mine.

Sometimes, when I'm the last one awake, when Lyle and Claire are fast asleep and the logs in the fireplace have burned down to embers, I'll curl up in front of the TV and pop in one of the tapes, looking for things I might have missed, or things I thought I'd only imagined. I've noticed, for instance, that when we first saw my father, when he embraced us at the Drome, he continued to hold Claire long after he'd turned me loose. It's as if the arc of our whole visit were inscribed in

208

that initial moment, plainly visible if you knew what to look for. To me, this is comforting. There's no beating fate.

For his part, my father's never mentioned the tapes. Possibly he thinks I destroyed them. Possibly he thinks I still have them. Possibly he's decided to let me keep them, now that he's able to see Claire every day. Shortly after we left Indianapolis, he sold his Bomber, broke his lease, and headed south. He took a room in an Econo Lodge over by Fort Jackson and proceeded to insinuate himself in our lives with a months-long campaign of charm and devotion. Eventually we agreed to rent him the cottage, and now, after years of not knowing where he was, I can look out my window, across a field where I played as a child, to the house my parents lived in when I was born, and see his floodlight burning in the night.

If he misses figure-eight racing and the closeness he felt to my mother, he doesn't complain. Perhaps it's enough to be back in the house they once shared. On weekends, he helps out at the mall. At first he refused to let me pay him, but now he just turns around and puts the money into a savings account for Claire, which he set up after I stopped accepting his checks. Afternoons, when the two of them aren't on the track down by the bluff, they're often at his workshop in the barn, where he builds kart engines. Claire's in charge of teaching him to use a computer. She's also in charge of worrying about him. For instance, she dislikes the idea of him traveling alone. This fall, he's been invited to the annual meeting of the Calorie Restriction Society in Phoenix, where he'll tell his story to a group of doctors, researchers, and fellow would-be Ponce de Leons. He's even managed to get my husband on the bandwagon. After just five weeks of CR, Lyle reports feeling better than he's felt in years. I used to think

CR was a crock, but these days I'm not so sure. The ability to do more with less is a valuable one, and it's not such a leap to believe our bodies know this. The body is, after all, geared for survival, capable of defending itself in unexpected ways, not so different from figure-eight racers, mothers protecting their young, the human heart itself.

ACKNOWLEDGMENTS

This book was more than eight years in the making. Along the way, I had a lot of help. My deepest gratitude goes to Julie Barer, as good a friend as an agent (which is saying a lot), and to my editor, Wylie O'Sullivan, who is even more wonderful than her name. I'm also indebted to Wylie's many hardworking colleagues at Free Press, notably Dominick Anfuso, Martha Levin, Jill Siegel, Carisa Hays, Suzanne Donahue, Shannon Gallagher, Wendy Sheanin, Carol de Onís, Beth Maglione, Erich Hobbing, Eric Fuentecilla, and Alex Noya.

Thanks and love to my mom, who's been there always, and to my dad, who graciously allowed his stories to be hijacked herein, which means more to me than he knows; to my aunt Dargan, who had answers; to Richard and Joanne and Jennifer, in-laws extraordinaire; to Dick and Lois Rosenthal, for their friendship, kindness, and for taking a chance on me; to Jeff Weiser, patron of the arts and the best friend I could want; to Judy Clain, for her advocacy and friendship; to Jeff MacGregor and Olya Evanitsky, who went above and beyond the call; to Lizzie Himmel, for making it fun; to Emily Watson, for bringing me into the circle; to the Bread Loaf Writers' Conference, for the privilege of waiting tables; to my unwitting teachers, the many fine writers whose work

I had the privilege of editing at *Story*; and to my witting teachers, especially Mary Grimm, Michelle Herman, and, of course, Lee K. Abbott, whose fault it is I write.

I'm also indebted to the magazine editors who originally published portions of this book: Rebecca Burns, Brock Clarke, Michael Ray, R. T. Smith, Hannah Tinti, Nancy Zafris, Linda Swanson-Davies, and Susan Burmeister-Brown. For their financial support, I'm grateful to the Arts Council of Indianapolis, the Indiana Arts Commission, and the Ohio Arts Council.

To the participants and staff of the Squaw Valley Community of Writers, I offer my heartfelt thanks for your unfailing friendship, generosity, and encouragement. I have never been so happy or so proud to be affiliated with a group of people.

Most of all, thank you, Deborah—for your brilliant, fierce editing; for your faith and support; for Hazel; for your love.

What You Have Left

A NOVEL

WILL ALLISON

Reading Group Guide

Author Q&A

ABOUT THIS GUIDE

The following reading group guide and author interview are intended to help you find interesting and rewarding approaches to your reading of *What You Have Left*. We hope these enhance your enjoyment and appreciation of the book.

READING GROUP GUIDE

1. This book doesn't start at the beginning of the story. Why do you think the author sometimes showed you the results of a character's actions before revealing his or her personal history? How might it have changed your ideas about Wylie if we read his side of the story first? How were your feelings about Cal affected by this structure?

2. The only two chapters in the novel that are narrated in the first person are chapter 3 (Lyle 1991) and chapter 8 (Holly 2007). Did it feel different to hear the characters speak for themselves in those chapters, rather than hearing their stories from a third-person narrator? How reliable are Holly and Lyle as narrators? Were there any specific passages that stood out to you in these chapters as particularly unreliable?

3. Discuss the relationship between Wylie and Lyle. Why did Lyle initially lie about having met Wylie (p. 67)? Do you think he had Holly's best interests in mind, or his own? What about his decision to switch car keys with Holly at the end of chapter 3 (p. 77) and take the blame when the police arrive? Was this an act of chivalry, or of self-interest?

4. In chapter 2 (Wylie 1971), we learn about the tragedy that befell Gladys and Lester's new baby, Nat. How do Gladys and Lester act as foils for Maddy and Wylie? Could what happened to baby Nat ever have happened to baby Holly? What evidence can you find that Wylie and Lester are different kinds of fathers? What suggests they are similar?

5. Did you view Wylie's decision to leave Holly with Cal as a selfish, or selfless, act? Is he fit for single parenthood? How do you think Holly's life would have been different if Wylie had raised her? How would *she* be different?

6. Lyle works in construction, and there are long, detailed passages about the projects he undertakes. How do these descriptions act as metaphors for his relationships in the book? As he is renovating Cal's home (p. 8), how is this reflected in his relationship with Holly? What about in his relationship with Cal? When he is reinforcing the foundation of the statehouse (p. 112), does the foundation of his relationship with Holly undergo any simultaneous renovation?

7. The walls of Cal's bedroom are made of pecky cypress, a desirable kind of wood that was once considered trash. "What makes pecky hard to find . . . is that you can't tell if a cypress is infected until you chop down the tree and cut it open (p. 6)." How is the pecky cypress like the Alzheimer's that runs in Cal's family? Why is it meaningful that Cal got the pecky cypress from the scrap pile at his father's sawmill?

8. Is it significant for you that Wylie and Maddy's relationship began while each of them was dating somebody else? How did learning about Dale and Sheila affect how you felt about Wylie and Maddy? Do you think they were really committed to one another?

9. Many of the characters in the novel battle addictions. What are some of the addictions the characters struggle with? Did any characters succeed in overcoming their addictions? How did the addictive personalities of the characters affect their relationships?

10. An interest in car racing seems to be almost genetic in the novel. How do the characters use their mutual interest in racing to remain close to one another? How does it pull them apart? What did you see as Maddy's primary obstacles? Did she really have to stop racing when she had Holly? How did the sexism she endured affect her relationship to the sport? Do you think racing will play a role in Claire's future, and, if so, will she have to face the same issues her grandmother faced?

11. When Holly and Wylie are finally reunited in chapter 8 (Holly 2007), Wylie's short-term memory has been jeopardized as the result of a seizure caused by a lifetime of drinking. He is convinced that he tried to contact Holly in recent years but got no response. Holly realizes that without the benefit of short-term memory, he is simply believing what he would like to be true. In this circumstance, is it the thought that counts? Do you believe that Wylie does in fact wish he had contacted Holly sooner?

12. How does car racing act as a metaphor for the relationships in the story? Which ones are going around in endless circles? Who is leading the race in different chapters? Who is trailing behind? Which relationships are more like Wylie's figure-8 races, characters just dodging a head-on collision?

13. Why did Holly steal Wylie's videotapes of his visit with her and Claire (p. 208)? Was this a final act of vengeance against the father that left her? Or did she want the tapes for herself and Claire? Will Wylie even remember?

14. At the end of *What You Have Left,* what do the characters have left? Is Wylie's memory loss a curse, or a blessing in disguise? Do Lyle and Holly have each other? Does Claire have everything she needs? Are you hopeful for the future of this family?

A CONVERSATION
WITH WILL ALLISON
by Claudia Labin

Did you know right away that it was Holly's story you wanted to tell?
Actually, her dad, Wylie, was the focal character of the first chapter I wrote, which appears in the book as chapter 7. It wasn't until I wrote a couple more chapters that Holly emerged as the protagonist. I didn't really have a plan. All I knew was that Wylie and Holly eventually would meet again.

How hard was it to give birth to this novel?
Harder than I expected. Back in college, I imagined I'd publish my first book in my twenties. Now, at thirty-nine, I'm just grateful this one made it out into the world.

Which of your characters was the most difficult to write?
Holly's grandfather, Cal, was tough. I'd already tried and failed once with a similar character in a short story. Like Cal, my grandfather had Alzheimer's, owned a dairy farm in South Carolina, etc. But the book required that Cal be an altogether different person than my grandfather. It took me a while to differentiate the two.

Author Q&A

In the book you take chances and make bold shifts in viewpoint and time. Could you explain what led you to switch between first- third-person point of view?
The book ended up with three chapters in first person and five in third person. The decisions were intuitive; I was just looking for the viewpoint that worked best for any given chapter. At some point or another, I think I tried all of them in both first and third.

Often, when I'm having trouble writing, switching viewpoint is what unlocks the story for me. It has to do with voice, obviously, but also with narrative distance, and tone, and how information is released.

How did your method of working on the short story differ from your method of working on the novel?
In the case of *What You Have Left,* not much, since the chapters are self-contained. But now that I'm working on a novel with a more conventional structure, I find myself planning more. The book is in the first person and proceeds chronologically, which means, in terms of structure, I have fewer ways of getting out of a jam; I can't switch to another character's viewpoint or jump around in time. So I feel a stronger need to have a sense of where the story is headed. I end up making a lot of notes about what's going to happen later in the book, or at least what might happen.

Did you show the manuscript to others during the drafting stages, before you showed it to an editor?
My wife, Deborah Way, is an editor at a magazine in New York. We met in the MFA program at Ohio State, and since then she's spent countless hours editing my fiction. As an

editor, she's very thorough, has very high expectations, and takes my work very seriously, which is exactly what I think every writer needs. I do, at least.

My agent, Julie Barer, also made several helpful suggestions before we sent the manuscript out.

In your acknowledgements at the end of the book, you thank your dad "who graciously allowed his stories to be hijacked." Are any of the characters based on real people? Was your dad a NASCAR aficionado?
None of the characters are based on real people, but a lot of the things that happen in the book happened to people I know. For instance, parts of Maddy's childhood are loosely based on stories my dad told me about his childhood. He's also the reason auto racing is in the book. He'd been friends with Cale Yarborough in high school and volunteered as a track steward at Columbia Speedway in the 1960s. When my brother and I were kids, he used to take us to the races.

Who would you say influenced you as a writer?
A great deal of what I know about writing—and reading, for that matter—I learned from Lee K. Abbott, whose workshops and literature courses I took as an undergraduate at Case Western and, later, as an MFA student at Ohio State. Mary Grimm and Michelle Herman were wonderful, generous teachers, too. I'm also indebted to the authors I worked with at *Story*. Reading and editing their work was an education in and of itself.

How has the Community of Writers at Squaw Valley impacted your writing?
I've had the good fortune of being a staff member at Squaw

Valley off and on since 1999, when I was still at *Story*. At first I thought it was corny that they called it a "community" instead of a conference, but I quickly came to regard it as the most important community in my writing life.

I think writers have a built-in need to get together. Most writers I know are very social people, yet we spend a big chunk of our lives alone at a desk, shut off from the rest of the world. It's good to come out of the cave and meet each other now and then. And of course it's helpful, professionally, to spend time with such an accomplished group of writers, editors, agents, etc. But the big thing about Squaw is the friendships I've made. Also, the valley itself is stunningly beautiful, and I like staying in a house with a bidet.

You were executive editor of *Story*. What did you look for when you got that stack of stories in the mail each day? And how, in the end, did the job impact your own writing?

I looked for stories that I couldn't put down, that were written with authority, and that in some way (voice, language, subject matter) stood out from others in the slush pile. Intelligent stories with a lot of heart. It didn't hurt if they were funny, or sad, or funny *and* sad. It especially didn't hurt if the author was unpublished, because we took a lot of pride in discovering new writers. Most of all, though, I just wanted to be moved.

Working at *Story* was very humbling. We got almost 20,000 submissions a year, and every day I was reading stories I liked better than mine—and rejecting most of them. The job gave me a fuller sense of the range and quality of fiction being written today, and it made me demand a lot more from myself as a writer.

Author Q&A

Where do you write?

I have a nice little office at home that Deborah dreams of turning into a bathroom. There's an old wooden desk, a metal chair on wheels. Usually the cat's in my lap, at least until my leg falls asleep.

John Updike apparently has three desks. Do you use different physical places to create, write, and edit?

Mostly I write on the computer at my desk, but I do find it useful to revise on a hard copy, somewhere other than in my office. Reading the words on an actual page helps me see problems I missed on the computer screen. Somehow the change of scenery helps too.

Also, I spend about 90 minutes a day driving my daughter to and from school. I do a lot of brainstorming in the car, talking into a handheld digital recorder.

How would you define yourself as a writer?

I'm just trying to tell a good story and write a book that readers will enjoy. If I manage to do that, I feel like I'm doing my job.

Reprinted with the kind permission of *The South Carolina Review*.

Long
Drive
Home

A NOVEL

WILL ALLISON

Dear Sara,

It's hard for me to imagine the person you'll be when you read this—probably on your way to college and a life of your own. Sometimes that feels like forever away. But other times—when you get into the car wearing your mom's perfume, or shush me distractedly as you study the menu at a diner, or manage to throw a baseball that goes exactly where you want it to—I feel time racing by so fast I can hardly breathe. Not knowing where things will stand between us ten years from now or how this letter will change them, I need to make sure you understand, before I go any further, how grateful I am to have you in my life, how lucky I am to be your father, how sorry I am for the way things have turned out between your mom and me since the accident. I know it's been hard. I know it's been confusing. My intention here is to be honest with you about all of it, to write down for later all the things I can't very well tell an eight-year-old now.

You may be wondering why I'm doing this. I won't pretend I'm not hoping you'll forgive me, but please don't think I'm asking for forgiveness, or that I think I deserve it. Detective Rizzo once told me that all confessions boil down to one thing: stress. People confess, he said, to relieve the psychological and physiological effects of guilt, regret, anxiety, shame. To share the burden with someone else. To at least glimpse the possibility of redemption. It's only human nature.

Remember the time you spilled orange juice on my keyboard and I didn't know why it wasn't working and you told me what you'd done, even though you could have gotten away with it? You said you couldn't stop thinking about it. You said you felt so bad, you had to tell me, even if you got in trouble. That's where I am. People confess when their need for relief overrides their instinct for self-preservation. I don't claim to be any different.

Still, I'm not sure I'd be writing this if I didn't also believe that, on some level, you already know the truth about the accident. You were there, after all. I have to think someday it's all going to come clear to you, and when it does, you'll know not only why I did what I did, but also that I wasn't honest with you about it. You don't deserve to be lied to. I don't want that between us, not on top of everything else. I don't want to make the same mistakes with you that I made with your mom.

Things didn't have to turn out the way they did. The accident was no more a matter of destiny than anything else you can rightfully call an accident, just mistakes and poor judgment. With a different choice here or there—and I'm talking the small ones you wouldn't otherwise give a second thought to—I could have gotten us safely home from school like I did every other day. Sara would have done her homework at the kitchen table while I prepped dinner, then we might have gone for a bike ride over to Ivy Hill Park, or played catch in the backyard, or worked on a jigsaw puzzle. She'd have kept me company in the basement while I folded laundry, or read a book on the rug in my office while I returned calls and checked email. At 6:38 sharp, we'd have gotten back into the station wagon to go meet Liz's train, then the three of us would have sat down to stir fry or spaghetti and meatballs and talked about the positions Liz was trying to fill at the bank, or whose parents we wanted to spend Thanksgiving with. Mostly, though, we'd have talked about Sara—which one of her friends she wanted the next play date with, what she wanted to be for Halloween, whether she was going to keep growing her hair or get it chopped off. Putting her to bed, Liz and I might even have paused to remark on how lucky we were, as we were inclined to do, but at no point would we have considered the possibility that we'd dodged a bullet that day, that we'd come *this close* to our lives veering permanently off course. That's the kind of thing you see only in hindsight.

ABOUT THE AUTHOR

WILL ALLISON'S debut novel, *What You Have Left,* was selected for Barnes & Noble Discover Great New Writers, Borders Original Voices, and Book Sense Picks, and was named one of 2007's notable books by the *San Francisco Chronicle.* His short stories have appeared in magazines such as *Zoetrope: All-Story, Glimmer Train,* and *One Story* and have received special mention in the *Pushcart Prize* and *Best American Short Stories* anthologies. He is the former executive editor of *Story.* Born in Columbia, South Carolina, he now lives with his wife and daughter in New Jersey. Learn more about Will Allison at www.willallison.com.